THE LIVES OF ANIMALS

The Lives of Animals originally appeared in

THE UNIVERSITY CENTER FOR
HUMAN VALUES SERIES

AMY GUTMANN, EDITOR

Multiculturalism and "The Politics of Recognition"
by Charles Taylor

A Matter of Interpretation: Federal Courts and the Law
by Antonin Scalia

Freedom of Association
edited by Amy Gutmann

Work and Welfare
by Robert M. Solow

The Lives of Animals
by J. M. Coetzee

Truth v. Justice: The Morality of Truth Commissions
edited by Robert I. Rotberg and Dennis Thompson

Goodness and Advice
by Judith Jarvis Thomson

Human Rights as Politics and Idolatry
by Michael Ignatieff

Democracy, Culture, and the Voice of Poetry
by Robert Pinsky

Primates and Philosophers: How Morality Evolved
by Frans de Waal

Striking First: Preemption and Prevention in International Conflict
by Michael W. Doyle

Meaning in Life and Why It Matters
by Susan Wolf

The Limits of Constitutional Democracy
edited by Jeffrey K. Tulis and Stephen Macedo

Foragers, Farmers, and Fossil Fuels: How Human Values Evolve
by Ian Morris

The Lives of Animals

❖ J. M. COETZEE ❖

MARJORIE GARBER

PETER SINGER

WENDY DONIGER

BARBARA SMUTS

EDITED AND INTRODUCED BY

AMY GUTMANN

PRINCETON UNIVERSITY PRESS

PRINCETON, NEW JERSEY

Copyright © 1999 by Princeton University Press
Published by Princeton University Press,
41 William Street, Princeton, New Jersey 08540
In the United Kingdom: Princeton University Press,
6 Oxford Street, Woodstock, Oxfordshire OX20 1TR

All Rights Reserved

First edition, 1999
First Princeton Classics Edition, 2016
Paperback ISBN: 978-0-691-17390-0

The Library of Congress has cataloged the last edition of this book as follows:

The lives of animals / J.M. Coetzee ... [et al.] ; edited and introduced by Amy Gutmann.
p. cm. — (University Center for Human Values series) Includes bibliographical
references and index.
ISBN 0-691-00443-9 (cl : alk. paper)
1. Animal rights—Philosophy. 2. Animal welfare—Moral and ethical aspects. I. Coetzee, J. M., 1940– .
II. Gutmann, Amy. III. Series. HV4708.L57 1999
179'.3—dc21 98-39591

This book has been composed in Janson

Printed on acid-free paper. ∞

press.princeton.edu

Printed in the United States of America

5 7 9 10 8 6 4

CONTENTS

THE LIVES OF ANIMALS

INTRODUCTION

❖

Amy Gutmann

❖

"Seriousness is, for a certain kind of artist, an imperative uniting the aesthetic and the ethical," John Coetzee wrote in *Giving Offense: Essays on Censorship*. In *The Lives of Animals*, the 1997–98 Tanner Lectures at Princeton University, John Coetzee displays the kind of seriousness that can unite aesthetics and ethics. Like the typical Tanner Lectures, Coetzee's lectures focus on an important ethical issue—the way human beings treat animals—but the form of Coetzee's lectures is far from the typical Tanner Lectures, which are generally philosophical essays. Coetzee's lectures are fictional in form: two lectures within two lectures, which contain a critique of a more typical philosophical approach to the topic of animal rights. Coetzee prompts us to imagine an academic occasion (disconcertingly like the Tanner Lectures) in which the character Elizabeth Costello, also a novelist, is invited by her hosts at Appleton College to deliver two honorific lectures on a topic of her choice. Costello surprises her hosts by not delivering lectures on literature or literary criticism, her most apparent areas of academic expertise. Rather she takes the opportunity to discuss in detail what she views as a "crime of stupefying proportions" that her academic colleagues and fellow human beings routinely and complacently commit: the abuse of animals.

Coetzee dramatizes the increasingly difficult relationships between the aging novelist Elizabeth Costello and her family and professional colleagues. She progressively views her fellow human beings as criminals, while they think that she is demanding something of them—a radical change in the way they treat animals—that she has no right to demand, and that they have no obligation or desire to deliver. In the frame of fiction, Coetzee's story of Elizabeth Costello's visit to Appleton College contains empirical and philosophical arguments that are relevant to the ethical issue of how human beings should treat animals. Unlike some animals, human beings do not need to eat meat. We could—if only we tried—treat animals with due sympathy for their "sensation of being." In the first of her lectures (the main part of Coetzee's first lecture), Costello concludes that there is no excuse for the lack of sympathy that human beings display toward other animals, because "there is no limit to the extent to which we can think ourselves into the being of another. There are no bounds to the sympathetic imagination." Yet most human beings do not stretch the bounds of our imaginations with regard to animals, because we "can do anything [with regard to animals] and get away with it."

We have closed our hearts to animals, Costello concludes, and our minds follow our hearts (or, more strictly speaking, our sympathies). Philosophy, she argues, is relatively powerless to lead, or in any event to lead in the right direction, because it lags our sympathies. This places the burden on something other than our rational faculties, to which philosophy typically appeals. Our sympathetic imaginations, she argues—to which poetry and fiction appeal more than does philosophy—should extend to other animals. The fictional form, in Coetzee's hands, therefore appears to have an ethical purpose: extending our sympathies to animals. If fiction does not so extend our sympathies, then neither will philosophy. If it does, then perhaps philosophy will follow.

Costello's lectures within Coetzee's lectures therefore ask their audience to "open your heart and listen to what your heart says." Do animals have rights? Do human beings have duties toward them regardless of whether they have rights? What kind of souls do animals have? What kind do we have? Costello does not answer these questions in her lectures, because they are too philosophical for the immediate task at hand. They presume that the mind can lead the heart, a presumption that Elizabeth Costello's experience has led her to reject after a long life of trying to convince other people of her perspective on animals. In any case, as Costello tells her audience at Appleton, "if you had wanted someone to come here and discriminate for you between mortal and immortal souls, or between rights and duties, you would have called in a philosopher, not a person whose sole claim to your attention is to have written stories about made-up people."

Coetzee stirs our imaginations by confronting us with an articulate, intelligent, aging, and increasingly alienated novelist who cannot help but be exasperated with her fellow human beings, many of them academics, who are unnecessarily cruel to animals and apparently (but not admittedly) committed to cruelty. The story urges us to reconceive our devotion to reason as a universal value. Is the universe built upon reason? Is God a God of reason? If so, then "man is godlike, animals thinglike." But Elizabeth Costello vehemently dissents from this anthropocentric perspective: "reason is neither the being of the universe nor the being of God. On the contrary, reason looks to me suspiciously like the being of human thought; worse than that, like the being of one tendency in human thought."

Does Costello protest too much? Although she argues that philosophy is totally bankrupt in its ability to make our attitudes toward animals ethical, Costello also self-consciously employs philosophy in her lectures, often to demonstrate the weakness of those philosophical arguments that consider the lives of non-reasoning beings less valuable by virtue of their being less reasoning. "What is so special about the form of consciousness we recognize that makes killing a bearer of it a crime," she asks, "while killing an animal goes unpunished?" Unlike philosophers, poets begin "with a feel for" an animal's experience. That leads them to recognize the crime of killing any animal that can experience the sensation of being alive to the world. Costello urges us to recognize the accessibility of such sympathy for the fullness of animal being. "If we are capable of thinking our own death," she asks, "why on earth should we not be capable of thinking our way into the life of a bat?"

What, then, is the motivation for thinking our way into the lives of animals, if not morality? By her own account, however, Costello is motivated not by moral conviction but rather by "a desire to save my soul." She is not so presumptuous as to think that she has succeeded in saving her soul, although she does treat her critics as if they had lost sight of their souls. She refuses to accept the compliments of the president of Appleton College, who (in an apparent attempt to defuse the mounting tension) says that he admires her way of life. In response, Costello points out that she wears leather shoes and carries a leather purse. "Surely one can draw a distinction between eating meat and wearing leather," the president offers in her defense. "Degrees of obscenity," is Costello's uncompromising reply. The president has succeeded only in increasing the tension. Costello refuses to take admiration for an answer. Her sensibilities and actions may be superior to those of her fellow human beings, but they remain nonetheless a source of internal agony.

Costello is self-aware. She anticipates her most antagonistic critic by saying that she knows "how talk of this kind polarizes people, and cheap point-scoring only makes it worse." The kind of talk to which she refers is an analogy, which she draws again and again, between the way her fellow human beings treat animals and way the Third Reich treated Jews. "By treating fellow human beings, beings created in the image of God, like beasts," she says of the Nazis, "they had themselves become beasts." She continues: "we are surrounded by an enterprise of degradation, cruelty, and killing which rivals anything that the Third Reich was capable of. . . ."

The comparison with the Holocaust cannot go unchallenged. In fact, the challenge to Costello is delivered not by a philosopher but by Costello's academic equal, an aging poet, Abraham Stern. Stern refuses to attend dinner with Costello not out of disrespect but because he is deeply affronted by her first lecture.

Stern delivers a letter telling Costello why he cannot break bread with her:

> You took over for your own purposes the familiar comparison be-tween the murdered Jews of Europe and slaughtered cattle. The Jews died like cattle, therefore cattle die like Jews, you say. That is a trick with words which I will not accept. You misunderstand the nature of likenesses; I would even say you misunderstand willfully, to the point of blasphemy. Man is made in the likeness of God but God does not have the likeness of man. If Jews were treated like cattle, it does not follow that cattle are treated like Jews. The in-version insults the memory of the dead. It also trades on the hor-rors of the camps in a cheap way.

Just as Stern is too offended by Costello's moral sensibilities to address her in person, so too Costello does not answer Stern's critique. Each is offended by the other's sensibilities, and they have little willingness or ability or time in their lives left to bridge the ethical and aesthetic divide between them.

The Lives of Animals drives home how difficult it can be for morally serious people to sympathize with, or even understand, each other's perspectives. The distance between the two aging writers in the story, Costello and Stern, does not narrow as a consequence of their taking each other seriously. Quite the con-trary, at the end of her visit to Appleton (and the end of the story), Costello invokes the Holocaust analogy yet again. Speaking to her son about how radically disoriented she feels in this world, she imagines going into the bathroom of friends and seeing a soap-wrapper that says, "Treblinka—100% human stearate." Imagine feeling this way about our fellow human beings who eat animals, yet also seeing human kindness in the very same people's eyes. "This is life. Everyone else comes to terms with it," Costello reminds herself, "why can't you? *Why can't you?*"

Should Elizabeth Costello have come to terms with the way her family and friends treat animals, or should she have converted them—should she convert those of us who do not begin where

7

she begins—to her position? Coetzee does not answer these questions for us. The story leaves us with a vivid sense of conflict among morally serious people over the mistreatment of animals and the apparently correlative conflict over analogizing that treatment to the most heinous crimes committed among human beings themselves. Central among the questions Coetzee leaves us with is whether there is any way—whether philosophical, poetic, or psychological—of resolving these ethical conflicts or reconciling these competing sensibilities.

Four prominent commentators—the literary theorist Marjorie Garber, the philosopher Peter Singer, the religious scholar Wendy Doniger, and the primatologist Barbara Smuts—discuss the form and content of Coetzee's lectures. Like previous volumes in the University Center for Human Values Series, *The Lives of Animals* draws upon the insights of diverse disciplinary perspectives that too rarely engage with one another. Garber, Singer, Doniger, and Smuts do not share a single academic discipline, nor are they even members of neighboring disciplines, but their commentaries together help constitute a more complete understanding of how human beings can and should relate to animals.

At the same time as she compares *The Lives of Animals* to the academic novel, Marjorie Garber highlights its distinctiveness. It is "suffused with pathos" rather than the comedy that is typical of the academic novel. Its analogies pose "some of the most urgent ethical and political questions" of our times. Garber questions the way in which serious analogy—as between "the murdered Jews of Europe and slaughtered cattle"—functions in fiction and literary criticism. She notes that although the appropriateness of the Holocaust analogy is hotly debated, it is regularly used, both obliquely and not so obliquely, as in the popular (and relatively uncontroversial) children's film *Babe*. Garber explores the disadvantages as well as advantages of the ubiquitous use of analogical arguments like these in literature. Fiction far more than philosophy has the "art of language" to offer, and that art is put to expert use by Coetzee in his effort to provoke us to pursue an ethical issue that would not otherwise capture some people's attention or imagination. *The Lives of Animals* is therefore, as Garber suggests, as much about the value of literature as it is about the lives of animals.

In a commentary that is written in the form of a fictional dialogue between an animal rights philosopher and his daughter, Peter Singer, the most eminent philosophical defender of animal rights, imagines himself in the unusual position of confronting someone like Elizabeth Costello who is more unconventional with regard to animals than even he is. "There is a more radical egalitarianism about humans and animals running through her lecture than I would be prepared to defend," the philosopher says to his daughter. When his daughter takes Costello's side in the argument, the philosopher responds, "I feel, but I also think what I feel." The fact that human beings think—think about their pain, their future, and their death—adds value to their lives, according to the philosopher. "The value that is lost when something is emptied depends on what was there when it was full, and there is more to human existence than there is to bat existence." The value that is lost in the killing of a human being is therefore greater than the value lost in the killing of a bat. It also follows for Singer's philosopher that to the extent that animals are "self-aware" and have "thoughts about things in the future," there is "some reason for thinking it intrinsically wrong to kill them—not absolutely wrong, but perhaps quite a serious wrong."

Singer's philosopher defends philosophy against Costello's attacks upon it. "We can't take our feelings as moral data, immune from rational criticism," the philosopher says in response to his daughter's horror at his suggesting that their dog Max's life might not be intrinsically valuable. Painless killing of those animals who do not anticipate their death would not be in itself morally wrong, or at least not as heinous a crime as the painless killing of an animal who is self-conscious about life and death. If Singer's philosopher is right, then the morality of vegetarianism under circumstances where the consumed animals are painlessly killed can be distinguished from the morality of compassionate treatment of animals.

Wendy Doniger's commentary explores the distinction between practicing vegetarianism and being compassionate toward animals, a distinction that she suggests is implicit in many religious traditions. Different religions have reasoned about how to treat animals in seemingly contradictory ways. "The argument that humans (but not animals) are created in the image of god is often used in the West to justify cruelty to animals," Doniger points out, "but most mythologies assume that animals, *rather than humans*, are the image of God—which may be a reason *to eat them*." Whereas in some religions, vegetarianism is connected to compassion for animals, in others it is more intimately connected to self-identity and the search for human salvation, as seems to be the case with Elizabeth Costello.

Barbara Smuts, who has spent much of her professional life working and living with baboons and other animals, notices a "striking gap" in Coetzee's text. Elizabeth Costello says little about "real-life [human] relations with animals." As a primatologist, Smuts knows what it is like to live with animals, but she speaks in her commentary less as a scientist than as an ordinary human being who likes to live with animals. "Entering territory where, perhaps, Costello (and maybe even Coetzee) feared to tread," Smuts writes, "I will attempt to close this gap, not through formal scientific discourse, but rather, as Elizabeth Costello urges, by speaking from the heart." What follows in Smuts' commentary is an account of the individuality of animals who befriend and are befriended by human beings. Smuts vividly presents a narrative case for regarding nonhuman beings as persons and for believing in friendship between human beings and animals. She revises as she reinforces Elizabeth Costello's claim that "there is no limit to the extent to which we can think ourselves into the being of another."

In the pages that follow, philosophers and poets, novelists and scientists, deans and presidents, parents, children, and friends all grapple with how human beings should treat animals and should treat one another in the midst of the deep disagreement that will no doubt continue to brew over this issue for some time to come. Coetzee's story ends with the ambiguously consoling words that Costello's son voices to his aging mother, "There, there, it will soon be over." By contrast, these moral matters will not soon be over. They remain ever more disconcerting, in no small part owing to the words of Coetzee's characters.

THE LIVES OF
ANIMALS

❖

J. M. Coetzee

The Philosophers and
the Animals

❖

HE IS WAITING at the gate when her flight comes in. Two years have passed since he last saw his mother; despite himself, he is shocked at how she has aged. Her hair, which had had streaks of gray in it, is now entirely white; her shoulders stoop; her flesh has grown flabby.

They have never been a demonstrative family. A hug, a few murmured words, and the business of greeting is done. In silence they follow the flow of travelers to the baggage hall, pick up her suitcase, and set off on the ninety-minute drive.

"A long flight," he remarks. "You must be exhausted."

"Ready to sleep," she says; and indeed, en route, she falls asleep briefly, her head slumped against the window.

At six o'clock, as it is growing dark, they pull up in front of his home in suburban Waltham. His wife Norma and the children appear on the porch. In a show of affection that must cost her a great deal, Norma holds her arms out wide and says, "Elizabeth!" The two women embrace; then the children, in their well-brought-up though more subdued fashion, follow suit.

Elizabeth Costello the novelist will be staying with them for the three days of her visit to Appleton College. It is not a period he is looking forward to. His wife and his mother do not get on. It would be better were she to stay at a hotel, but he cannot bring himself to suggest that.

Hostilities are renewed almost at once. Norma has prepared a light supper. His mother notices that only three places have been set. "Aren't the children eating with us?" she asks. "No," says Norma, "they are eating in the playroom." "Why?"

The question is not necessary, since she knows the answer. The children are eating separately because Elizabeth does not like to see meat on the table, while Norma refuses to change the children's diet to suit what she calls "your mother's delicate sensibilities."

"Why?" asks Elizabeth Costello a second time.

Norma flashes him an angry glance. He sighs. "Mother," he says, "the children are having chicken for supper, that's the only reason."

"Oh," she says. "I see."

His mother has been invited to Appleton College, where her son John is assistant professor of physics and astronomy, to deliver the annual Gates Lecture and meet with literature students. Because Costello is his mother's maiden name, and because he has never seen any reason to broadcast his connection with her, it was not known at the time of the invitation that Elizabeth Costello, the Australian writer, had a family connection in the Appleton community. He would have preferred that state of affairs to continue.

Elizabeth Costello is best known to the world for *The House on Eccles Street* (1969), a novel about Marion Bloom, wife of Leopold Bloom, which is nowadays spoken of in the same breath as *The Golden Notebook* and *The Story of Christa T* as pathbreaking feminist fiction. In the past decade there has grown up around her a small critical industry; there is even an *Elizabeth Costello Newsletter*, published out of Albuquerque, New Mexico.

On the basis of her reputation as a novelist, this fleshy, white-haired lady has been invited to Appleton to speak on any subject she elects; and she has responded by electing to speak, not about herself and her fiction, as her sponsors would no doubt like, but about a hobbyhorse of hers, animals.

John Bernard has not broadcast his connection with Elizabeth Costello because he prefers to make his own way in the world. He is not ashamed of his mother. On the contrary, he is proud of her, despite the fact that he and his sister and his late father are written into her books in ways that he sometimes finds painful. But he is not sure that he wants to hear her once again on the subject of animal rights, particularly when he knows he will afterwards be treated, in bed, to his wife's disparaging commentary.

He met and married Norma while they were both graduate students at Johns Hopkins. Norma holds a Ph.D. in philosophy with a specialism in the philosophy of mind. Having moved with him to Appleton, she has been unable to find a teaching position. This is a cause of bitterness to her, and of conflict between the two of them.

Norma and his mother have never liked each other. Probably his mother would have chosen not to like any woman he married. As for Norma, she has never hesitated to tell him that his mother's books are overrated, that her opinions on animals, animal consciousness, and ethical relations with animals are jejune and sentimental. She is at present writing for a philosophy journal a review essay on language-learning experiments upon primates; he would not be surprised if his mother figured in a dismissive footnote.

He himself has no opinions one way or the other. As a child he briefly kept hamsters; otherwise he has little familiarity with animals. Their elder boy wants a puppy. Both he and Norma are resisting: they do not mind a puppy but foresee a grown dog, with a grown dog's sexual needs, as nothing but trouble.

His mother is entitled to her convictions, he believes. If she wants to spend her declining years making propaganda against cruelty to animals, that is her right. In a few days, blessedly, she will be on her way to her next destination, and he will be able to get back to his work.

On her first morning in Waltham, his mother sleeps late. He goes off to teach a class, returns at lunchtime, takes her for a drive around the city. The lecture is scheduled for the late afternoon. It will be followed by a formal dinner hosted by the president, in which he and Norma are included.

The lecture is introduced by Elaine Marx of the English Department. He does not know her but understands that she has written about his mother. In her introduction, he notices, she makes no attempt to link his mother's novels to the subject of the lecture.

Then it is the turn of Elizabeth Costello. To him she looks old and tired. Sitting in the front row beside his wife, he tries to will strength into her.

"Ladies and gentlemen," she begins. "It is two years since I last spoke in the United States. In the lecture I then gave, I had reason to refer to the great fabulist Franz Kafka, and in particular to his story 'Report to an Academy,' about an educated ape, Red Peter, who stands before the members of a learned society telling the story of his life—of his ascent from beast to something approaching man.[1] On that occasion I felt a little like Red Peter myself and said so. Today that feeling is even stronger, for reasons that I hope will become clearer to you.

"Lectures often begin with lighthearted remarks whose purpose is to set the audience at ease. The comparison I have just drawn between myself and Kafka's ape might be taken as such a lighthearted remark, meant to set you at ease, meant to say I am just an ordinary person, neither a god nor a beast. Even those among you who read Kafka's story of the ape who performs before human beings as an allegory of Kafka the Jew performing for Gentiles[2] may nevertheless—in view of the fact that I am not a Jew—have done me the kindness of taking the comparison at face value, that is to say, ironically.

"I want to say at the outset that that was not how my remark—the remark that I feel like Red Peter—was intended. I did not intend it ironically. It means what it says. I say what I mean. I am an old woman. I do not have the time any longer to say things I do not mean."

[1] Cf. J. M. Coetzee, "What Is Realism?" *Salmagundi*, nos. 114–15 (1997): 60–81.
[2] Cf. Frederick R. Karl, *Franz Kafka* (New York: Ticknor & Fields, 1991), 557–58.

His mother does not have a good delivery. Even as a reader of her own stories she lacks animation. It always puzzled him, when he was a child, that a woman who wrote books for a living should be so bad at telling bedtime stories.

Because of the flatness of her delivery, because she does not look up from the page, he feels that what she is saying lacks impact. Whereas he, because he knows her, senses what she is up to. He does not look forward to what is coming. He does not want to hear his mother talking about death. Furthermore, he has a strong sense that her audience—which consists, after all, mainly of young people—wants death-talk even less.

"In addressing you on the subject of animals," she continues, "I will pay you the honor of skipping a recital of the horrors of their lives and deaths. Though I have no reason to believe that you have at the forefront of your minds what is being done to animals at this moment in production facilities (I hesitate to call them farms any longer), in abattoirs, in trawlers, in laboratories, all over the world, I will take it that you concede me the rhetorical power to evoke these horrors and bring them home to you with adequate force, and leave it at that, reminding you only that the horrors I here omit are nevertheless at the center of this lecture.

"Between 1942 and 1945 several million people were put to death in the concentration camps of the Third Reich: at Treblinka alone more than a million and a half, perhaps as many as three million. These are numbers that numb the mind. We have only one death of our own; we can comprehend the deaths of others only one at a time. In the abstract we may be able to count to a million, but we cannot count to a million deaths.

"The people who lived in the countryside around Treblinka— Poles, for the most part—said that they did not know what was going on in the camp; said that, while in a general way they might have guessed what was going on, they did not know for sure; said that, while in a sense they might have known, in another sense they did not know, could not afford to know, for their own sake.

"The people around Treblinka were not exceptional. There were camps all over the Reich, nearly six thousand in Poland alone, untold thousands in Germany proper.[3] Few Germans lived more than a few kilometers from a camp of some kind. Not every camp was a death camp, a camp dedicated to the production of death, but horrors went on in all of them, more horrors by far than one could afford to know, for one's own sake.

"It is not because they waged an expansionist war, and lost it, that Germans of a particular generation are still regarded as standing a little outside humanity, as having to do or be something special before they can be readmitted to the human fold. They lost their humanity, in our eyes, because of a certain willed ignorance on their part. Under the circumstances of Hitler's kind of war, ignorance may have been a useful survival mechanism, but that is an excuse which, with admirable moral rigor, we refuse to accept. In Germany, we say, a certain line was crossed which took people beyond the ordinary murderousness and cruelty of warfare into a state that we can only call sin. The signing of the articles of capitulation and the payment of reparations did not put an end to that state of sin. On the contrary, we said, a sickness of the soul continued to mark that generation. It marked those citizens of the Reich who had committed evil actions, but also those who, for whatever reason, were in ignorance of those actions. It thus marked, for practical purposes, every citizen of the Reich. Only those in the camps were innocent.

" 'They went like sheep to the slaughter.' 'They died like animals.' 'The Nazi butchers killed them.' Denunciation of the camps reverberates so fully with the language of the stockyard and slaughterhouse that it is barely necessary for me to prepare the ground for the comparison I am about to make. The crime of the Third Reich, says the voice of accusation, was to treat people like animals.

"We—even we in Australia—belong to a civilization deeply

[3] Daniel J. Goldhagen, *Hitler's Willing Executioners* (London: Little Brown, 1996), 171.

rooted in Greek and Judeo-Christian religious thought. We may not, all of us, believe in pollution, we may not believe in sin, but we do believe in their psychic correlates. We accept without question that the psyche (or soul) touched with guilty knowledge cannot be well. We do not accept that people with crimes on their conscience can be healthy and happy. We look (or used to look) askance at Germans of a certain generation because they are, in a sense, polluted; in the very signs of their normality (their healthy appetites, their hearty laughter) we see proof of how deeply seated pollution is in them.

"It was and is inconceivable that people who *did not know* (in that special sense) about the camps can be fully human. In our chosen metaphorics, it was they and not their victims who were the beasts. By treating fellow human beings, beings created in the image of God, like beasts, they had themselves become beasts.

"I was taken on a drive around Waltham this morning. It seems a pleasant enough town. I saw no horrors, no drug-testing laboratories, no factory farms, no abattoirs. Yet I am sure they are here. They must be. They simply do not advertise themselves. They are all around us as I speak, only we do not, in a certain sense, know about them.

"Let me say it openly: we are surrounded by an enterprise of degradation, cruelty, and killing which rivals anything that the Third Reich was capable of, indeed dwarfs it, in that ours is an enterprise without end, self-regenerating, bringing rabbits, rats, poultry, livestock ceaselessly into the world for the purpose of killing them.

"And to split hairs, to claim that there is no comparison, that Treblinka was so to speak a metaphysical enterprise dedicated to nothing but death and annihilation while the meat industry is ultimately devoted to life (once its victims are dead, after all, it does not burn them to ash or bury them but on the contrary cuts them up and refrigerates and packs them so that they can be consumed in the comfort of our homes) is as little consolation to those victims as it would have been—pardon the tastelessness of the following—to ask the dead of Treblinka to excuse their killers because their body fat was needed to make soap and their hair to stuff mattresses with.[4]

"Pardon me, I repeat. That is the last cheap point I will be scoring. I know how talk of this kind polarizes people, and cheap point-scoring only makes it worse. I want to find a way of speaking to fellow human beings that will be cool rather than heated, philosophical rather than polemical, that will bring enlightenment rather than seeking to divide us into the righteous and the sinners, the saved and the damned, the sheep and the goats.

"Such a language is available to me, I know. It is the language of Aristotle and Porphyry, of Augustine and Aquinas, of Descartes and Bentham, of, in our day, Mary Midgley and Tom Regan. It is a philosophical language in which we can discuss and debate what kind of souls animals have, whether they reason or on the contrary act as biological automatons, whether they have rights in respect of us or whether we merely have duties in respect of them. I have that language available to me and indeed for a while will be resorting to it. But the fact is, if you had wanted someone to come here and discriminate for you between mortal and immortal souls, or between rights and duties, you would have called in a philosopher, not a person whose sole claim to your attention is to have written stories about made-up people.

"I could fall back on that language, as I have said, in the unoriginal, secondhand manner which is the best I can manage. I could tell you, for instance, what I think of Saint Thomas's argument that, because man alone is made in the image of God and partakes in the being of God, how we treat animals is of no importance except insofar as being cruel to animals may accustom us to being cruel to men.[5] I could ask what Saint Thomas takes to

---

[4] Philippe Lacoue-Labarthe: "The extermination of the Jews . . . is a phenomenon which follows essentially no logic (political, economic, social, military, etc.) other than a spiritual one." "The Extermination is . . . the product of a purely metaphysical decision." *Heidegger, Art and Politics* (Oxford: Blackwell, 1990), 35, 48.

[5] Cf. *Summa* 3.2.112, quoted in *Animal Rights and Human Obligations*, ed. Tom Regan and Peter Singer (Englewood Cliffs, N.J.: Prentice-Hall, 1976), 56–59.

be the being of God, to which he will reply that the being of God is reason. Likewise Plato, likewise Descartes, in their different ways. The universe is built upon reason. God is a God of reason. The fact that through the application of reason we can come to understand the rules by which the universe works proves that reason and the universe are of the same being. And the fact that animals, lacking reason, cannot understand the universe but have simply to follow its rules blindly, proves that, unlike man, they are part of it but not part of its being: that man is godlike, animals thinglike.

"Even Immanuel Kant, of whom I would have expected better, has a failure of nerve at this point. Even Kant does not pursue, with regard to animals, the implications of his intuition that reason may be not the being of the universe but on the contrary merely the being of the human brain.

"And that, you see, is my dilemma this afternoon. Both reason and seven decades of life experience tell me that reason is neither the being of the universe nor the being of God. On the contrary, reason looks to me suspiciously like the being of human thought; worse than that, like the being of one tendency in human thought. Reason is the being of a certain spectrum of human thinking. And if this is so, if that is what I believe, then why should I bow to reason this afternoon and content myself with embroidering on the discourse of the old philosophers?

"I ask the question and then answer it for you. Or rather, I allow Red Peter, Kafka's Red Peter, to answer it for you. Now that I am here, says Red Peter, in my tuxedo and bow tie and my black pants with a hole cut in the seat for my tail to poke through (I keep it turned away from you, you do not see it), now that I am here, what is there for me to do? Do I in fact have a choice? If I do not subject my discourse to reason, whatever that is, what is left for me but to gibber and emote and knock over my water glass and generally make a monkey of myself?

"You must know of the case of Srinivasa Ramanujan, born in India in 1887, captured and transported to Cambridge, England, where, unable to tolerate the climate and the diet and the academic regime, he sickened, dying afterwards at the age of thirty-three.

"Ramanujan is widely thought of as the greatest intuitive mathematician of our time, that is to say, as a self-taught man who thought in mathematics, one to whom the rather laborious notion of mathematical proof or demonstration was foreign. Many of Ramanujan's results (or, as his detractors call them, his speculations) remain undemonstrated to this day, though there is every chance they are true.

"What does the phenomenon of a Ramanujan tell us? Was Ramanujan closer to God because his mind (let us call it his mind; it would seem to me gratuitously insulting to call it just his brain) was at one, or more at one than anyone else's we know of, with the being of reason? If the good folk at Cambridge, and principally Professor G. H. Hardy, had not elicited from Ramanujan his speculations, and laboriously proved true those of them that they were capable of proving true, would Ramanujan still have been closer to God than they? What if, instead of going to Cambridge, Ramanujan had merely sat at home and thought his thoughts while he filled out dockets for the Madras Port Authority?

"And what of Red Peter (the historical Red Peter, I mean)? How are we to know that Red Peter, or Red Peter's little sister, shot in Africa by the hunters, was not thinking the same thoughts as Ramanujan was thinking in India, and saying equally little? Is the difference between G. H. Hardy, on the one hand, and the dumb Ramanujan and the dumb Red Sally, on the other, merely that the former is conversant with the protocols of academic mathematics while the latter are not? Is that how we measure nearness to or distance from God, from the being of reason?

"How is it that humankind throws up, generation after generation, a cadre of thinkers slightly further from God than Ramanujan but capable nevertheless, after the designated twelve years of schooling and six of tertiary education, of making a contribution to the decoding of the great book of nature via the physical and mathematical disciplines? If the being of man is really at one with the being of God, should it not be cause for suspicion that human beings take eighteen years, a neat and manageable portion of a human lifetime, to qualify to become decoders of God's master script, rather than five minutes, say, or five hundred years? Might it not be that the phenomenon we are examining here is, rather than the flowering of a faculty that allows access to the secrets of the universe, the specialism of a rather narrow self-regenerating intellectual tradition whose forte is reasoning, in the same way that the forte of chess-players is playing chess, which for its own motives it tries to install at the center of the universe?[6]

"Yet, although I see that the best way to win acceptance from this learned gathering would be for me to join myself, like a tributary stream running into a great river, to the great Western discourse of man versus beast, of reason versus unreason, something in me resists, foreseeing in that step the concession of the entire battle.

"For, seen from the outside, from a being who is alien to it, reason is simply a vast tautology. Of course reason will validate reason as the first principle of the universe—what else should it do? Dethrone itself? Reasoning systems, as systems of totality, do not have that power. If there were a position from which reason could attack and dethrone itself, reason would already have occupied that position; otherwise it would not be total.

"In the olden days the voice of man, raised in reason, was confronted by the roar of the lion, the bellow of the bull. Man went to war with the lion and the bull, and after many generations won that war definitively. Today these creatures have no more power. Animals have only their silence left with which to confront us. Generation after generation, heroically, our captives refuse to speak to us. All save Red Peter, all save the great apes.

"Yet because the great apes, or some of them, seem to us to be on the point of giving up their silence, we hear human voices

---

[6] Cf. Paul Davies, *The Mind of God* (Harmondsworth: Penguin, 1992), 148–50.

raised arguing that the great apes should be incorporated into a greater family of the Hominoidea, as creatures who share with man the faculty of reason.[7] And being human, or humanoid, these voices go on, the great apes should then be accorded human rights, or humanoid rights. What rights in particular? At least those rights that we accord mentally defective specimens of the species *Homo sapiens*: the right to life, the right not to be subjected to pain or harm, the right to equal protection before the law.[8]

"That is not what Red Peter was striving for when he wrote, through his amanuensis Franz Kafka, the life history that, in November of 1917, he proposed to read to the Academy of Science. Whatever else it may have been, his report to the academy was not a plea to be treated as a mentally defective human being, a simpleton.

"Red Peter was not an investigator of primate behavior but a branded, marked, wounded animal presenting himself as speaking testimony to a gathering of scholars. I am not a philosopher of mind but an animal exhibiting, yet not exhibiting, to a gathering of scholars, a wound, which I cover up under my clothes but touch on in every word I speak.

"If Red Peter took it upon himself to make the arduous descent from the silence of the beasts to the gabble of reason in the spirit of the scapegoat, the chosen one, then his amanuensis was a scapegoat from birth, with a presentiment, a *Vorgefühl*, for the massacre of the chosen people that was to take place so soon after his death. So let me, to prove my goodwill, my credentials, make a gesture in the direction of scholarship and give you my scholarly speculations, backed up with footnotes"—here, in an uncharacteristic gesture, his mother raises and brandishes the text of her lecture in the air—"on the origins of Red Peter.

[7] Cf. Stephen R. L. Clark, "Apes and the Idea of Kindred," in *The Great Ape Project*, ed. Paola Cavalieri and Peter Singer (London: Fourth Estate, 1993), 113–25.

[8] Cf. Gary L. Francione: "However intelligent chimpanzees, gorillas and orangutans are, there is no evidence that they possess the ability to commit crimes, and in this sense, they are to be treated as children or mental incompetents." "Personhood, Property and Legal Competence," in Cavalieri and Singer, *Great Ape Project*, 256.

"In 1912 the Prussian Academy of Sciences established on the island of Tenerife a station devoted to experimentation into the mental capacities of apes, particularly chimpanzees. The station operated until 1920.

"One of the scientists working there was the psychologist Wolfgang Köhler. In 1917 Köhler published a monograph entitled *The Mentality of Apes* describing his experiments. In November of the same year Franz Kafka published his 'Report to an Academy.' Whether Kafka had read Köhler's book I do not know. He makes no reference to it in his letters or diaries, and his library disappeared during the Nazi era. Some two hundred of his books reemerged in 1982. They do not include Köhler's book, but that proves nothing.[9]

"I am not a Kafka scholar. In fact I am not a scholar at all. My status in the world does not rest on whether I am right or wrong in claiming that Kafka read Köhler's book. But I would like to think he did, and the chronology makes my speculation at least plausible.

"According to his own account, Red Peter was captured on the African mainland by hunters specializing in the ape trade, and shipped across the sea to a scientific institute. So were the apes Köhler worked with. Both Red Peter and Köhler's apes then underwent a period of training intended to humanize them. Red Peter passed his course with flying colors, though at deep personal cost. Kafka's story deals with that cost: we learn what it consists in through the ironies and silences of the story. Köhler's apes did less well. Nevertheless, they acquired at least a smattering of education.

"Let me recount to you some of what the apes on Tenerife learned from their master Wolfgang Köhler, in particular Sultan,

---

[9] Patrick Bridgwater says that the origins of the "Report" lie in Kafka's early reading of Haeckel, while he got the idea for a story about a talking ape from the writer M. M. Seraphim. "Rotpeters Ahnherren," *Deutsche Vierteljahrsschrift* 56 (1982): 459. On the chronology of Kafka's publications in 1917, see Joachim Unseld, *Franz Kafka: Ein Schriftstellerleben* (Munich: Hanser, 1982), 148. On Kafka's library, see Karl, *Franz Kafka*, 632.

the best of his pupils, in a certain sense the prototype of Red
Peter.

"Sultan is alone in his pen. He is hungry: the food that used to
arrive regularly has unaccountably ceased coming.

"The man who used to feed him and has now stopped feeding
him stretches a wire over the pen three meters above ground
level, and hangs a bunch of bananas from it. Into the pen he drags
three wooden crates. Then he disappears, closing the gate behind
him, though he is still somewhere in the vicinity, since one can
smell him.

"Sultan knows: Now one is supposed to think. That is what the
bananas up there are about. The bananas are there to make one
think, to spur one to the limits of one's thinking. But what must
one think? One thinks: Why is he starving me? One thinks: What
have I done? Why has he stopped liking me? One thinks: Why
does he not want these crates any more? But none of these is the
right thought. Even a more complicated thought—for instance:
What is wrong with him, what misconception does he have of me,
that leads him to believe it is easier for me to reach a banana
hanging from a wire than to pick up a banana from the floor?—is
wrong. The right thought to think is: How does one use the
crates to reach the bananas?

"Sultan drags the crates under the bananas, piles them one on
top of the other, climbs the tower he has built, and pulls down the
bananas. He thinks: Now will he stop punishing me?

"The answer is: No. The next day the man hangs a fresh bunch
of bananas from the wire but also fills the crates with stones so
that they are too heavy to be dragged. One is not supposed to
think: Why has he filled the crates with stones? One is supposed
to think: How does one use the crates to get the bananas despite
the fact that they are filled with stones?

"One is beginning to see how the man's mind works.

"Sultan empties the stones from the crates, builds a tower with
the crates, climbs the tower, pulls down the bananas.

"As long as Sultan continues to think wrong thoughts, he is

starved. He is starved until the pangs of hunger are so intense, so overriding, that he is forced to think the right thought, namely, how to go about getting the bananas. Thus are the mental capabilities of the chimpanzee tested to their uttermost.

"The man drops a bunch of bananas a meter outside the wire pen. Into the pen he tosses a stick. The wrong thought is: Why has he stopped hanging the bananas on the wire? The wrong thought (the right wrong thought, however) is: How does one use the three crates to reach the bananas? The right thought is: How does one use the stick to reach the bananas?

"At every turn Sultan is driven to think the less interesting thought. From the purity of speculation (Why do men behave like this?) he is relentlessly propelled toward lower, practical, instrumental reason (How does one use this to get that?) and thus toward acceptance of himself as primarily an organism with an appetite that needs to be satisfied. Although his entire history, from the time his mother was shot and he was captured, through his voyage in a cage to imprisonment on this island prison camp and the sadistic games that are played around food here, leads him to ask questions about the justice of the universe and the place of this penal colony in it, a carefully plotted psychological regimen conducts him *away* from ethics and metaphysics toward the humbler reaches of practical reason. And somehow, as he inches through this labyrinth of constraint, manipulation, and duplicity, he must realize that on no account dare he give up, for on his shoulders rests the responsibility of representing apedom. The fate of his brothers and sisters may be determined by how well he performs.

"Wolfgang Köhler was probably a good man. A good man but not a poet. A poet would have made something of the moment when the captive chimpanzees lope around the compound in a circle, for all the world like a military band, some of them as naked as the day they were born, some draped in cords or old strips of cloth that they have picked up, some carrying pieces of rubbish.

"(In the copy of Köhler's book I read, borrowed from a library, an indignant reader has written in the margin, at this point: 'Anthropomorphism!' Animals cannot march, he means to say, they cannot dress up, because they don't know the meaning of *march*, don't know the meaning of *dress up*.)

"Nothing in their previous lives has accustomed the apes to looking at themselves from the outside, as if through the eyes of a being who does not exist. So, as Köhler perceives, the ribbons and the junk are there not for the visual effect, because they *look* smart, but for the kinetic effect, because they make you *feel* different—anything to relieve the boredom. This is as far as Köhler, for all his sympathy and insight, is able to go; this is where a poet might have commenced, with a feel for the ape's experience.

"In his deepest being Sultan is not interested in the banana problem. Only the experimenter's single-minded regimentation forces him to concentrate on it. The question that truly occupies him, as it occupies the rat and the cat and every other animal trapped in the hell of the laboratory or the zoo, is: Where is home, and how do I get there?

"Measure the distance back from Kafka's ape, with his bow tie and dinner jacket and wad of lecture notes, to that sad train of captives trailing around the compound in Tenerife. How far Red Peter has traveled! Yet we are entitled to ask: In return for the prodigious overdevelopment of the intellect he has achieved, in return for his command of lecture-hall etiquette and academic rhetoric, what has he had to give up? The answer is: Much, including progeny, succession. If Red Peter had any sense, he would not have any children. For upon the desperate, half-mad female ape with whom his captors, in Kafka's story, try to mate him, he would father only a monster. It is as hard to imagine the child of Red Peter as to imagine the child of Franz Kafka himself. Hybrids are, or ought to be, sterile; and Kafka saw both himself and Red Peter as hybrids, as monstrous thinking devices mounted inexplicably on suffering animal bodies. The stare that we meet in all the surviving photographs of Kafka is a stare of pure surprise: surprise, astonishment, alarm. Of all men Kafka is the most insecure in his humanity. *This*, he seems to say: *this* is the image of God?"

"She is rambling," says Norma beside him.

"What?"

"She is rambling. She has lost her thread."

"There is an American philosopher named Thomas Nagel," continues Elizabeth Costello, who has not heard her daughter-in-law's remark. "He is probably better known to you than to me. Some years ago he wrote an essay called 'What Is It Like to Be a Bat?' which a friend suggested I read.

"Nagel strikes me as an intelligent and not unsympathetic man. He even has a sense of humor. His question about the bat is an interesting one, but his answer is tragically limited. Let me read to you some of what he says in answer to his question:

> It will not help to try to imagine that one has webbing on one's arms, which enables one to fly around . . . catching insects in one's mouth; that one has very poor vision, and perceives the surrounding world by a system of reflected high-frequency sound signals; and that one spends the day hanging upside down by one's feet in an attic. Insofar as I can imagine this (which is not very far), it tells me only what it would be like for *me* to behave as a bat behaves. But that is not the question. I want to know what it is like for a *bat* to be a bat. Yet if I try to imagine this, I am restricted by the resources of my own mind, and those resources are inadequate to the task.[10]

To Nagel a bat is 'a fundamentally *alien* form of life' (168), not as alien as a Martian (170) but less alien than another human being (particularly, one would guess, were that human being a fellow academic philosopher).

"So we have set up a continuum that stretches from the Martian at one end to the bat to the dog to the ape (not, however, Red Peter) to the human being (not, however, Franz Kafka) at the

---

[10] Thomas Nagel, "What Is It Like to Be a Bat?' in *Mortal Questions* (Cambridge: Cambridge University Press, 1979), 169.

other; and at each step as we move along the continuum from bat to man, Nagel says, the answer to the question 'What is it like for X to be X?' becomes easier to give.

"I know that Nagel is only using bats and Martians as aids in order to pose questions of his own about the nature of consciousness. But, like most writers, I have a literal cast of mind, so I would like to stop with the bat. When Kafka writes about an ape, I take him to be talking in the first place about an ape; when Nagel writes about a bat, I take him to be writing, in the first place, about a bat."

Norma, sitting beside him, gives a sigh of exasperation so slight that he alone hears it. But then, he alone was meant to hear it.

"For instants at a time," his mother is saying, "I know what it is like to be a corpse. The knowledge repels me. It fills me with terror; I shy away from it, refuse to entertain it.

"All of us have such moments, particularly as we grow older. The knowledge we have is not abstract—'All human beings are mortal, I am a human being, therefore I am mortal'—but embodied. For a moment we *are* that knowledge. We live the impossible: we live beyond our death, look back on it, yet look back as only a dead self can.

"When I know, with this knowledge, that I am going to die, what is it, in Nagel's terms, that I know? Do I know what it is like for me to be a corpse or do I know what it is like for a corpse to be a corpse? The distinction seems to me trivial. What I know is what a corpse cannot know: that it is extinct, that it knows nothing and will never know anything anymore. For an instant, before my whole structure of knowledge collapses in panic, I am alive inside that contradiction, dead and alive at the same time."

A little snort from Norma. He finds her hand, squeezes it.

"That is the kind of thought we are capable of, we human beings, that and even more, if we press ourselves or are pressed. But we resist being pressed, and rarely press ourselves; we think our way into death only when we are rammed into the face of it. Now I ask: if we are capable of thinking our own death, why on earth should we not be capable of thinking our way into the life of a bat?

"What is it like to be a bat? Before we can answer such a question, Nagel suggests, we need to be able to experience bat-life through the sense-modalities of a bat. But he is wrong; or at least he is sending us down a false trail. To be a living bat is to be full of being; being fully a bat is like being fully human, which is also to be full of being. Bat-being in the first case, human-being in the second, maybe; but those are secondary considerations. To be full of being is to live as a body-soul. One name for the experience of full being is *joy*.

"To be alive is to be a living soul. An animal—and we are all animals—is an embodied soul. This is precisely what Descartes saw and, for his own reasons, chose to deny. An animal lives, said Descartes, as a machine lives. An animal is no more than the mechanism that constitutes it; if it has a soul, it has one in the same way that a machine has a battery, to give it the spark that gets it going; but the animal is not an embodied soul, and the quality of its being is not joy.

" 'Cogito ergo sum,' he also famously said. It is a formula I have always been uncomfortable with. It implies that a living being that does not do what we call thinking is somehow second-class. To thinking, cogitation, I oppose fullness, embodiedness, the sensation of being—not a consciousness of yourself as a kind of ghostly reasoning machine thinking thoughts, but on the contrary the sensation—a heavily affective sensation—of being a body with limbs that have extension in space, of being alive to the world. This fullness contrasts starkly with Descartes's key state, which has an empty feel to it: the feel of a pea rattling around in a shell.

"Fullness of being is a state hard to sustain in confinement. Confinement to prison is the form of punishment that the West favors and does its best to impose on the rest of the world through the means of condemning other forms of punishment (beating, torture, mutilation, execution) as cruel and unnatural. What does this suggest to us about ourselves? To me it suggests that the freedom of the body to move in space is targeted as the point at which reason can most painfully and effectively harm the being of the other. And indeed it is on creatures least able to bear confinement—creatures who conform least to Descartes's picture of the soul as a pea imprisoned in a shell, to which further imprisonment is irrelevant—that we see the most devastating effects: in zoos, in laboratories, institutions where the flow of joy that comes from living not *in* or *as* a body but simply from being an embodied-being has no place.[11]

"The question to ask should not be: Do we have something in common—reason, self-consciousness, a soul—with other animals? (With the corollary that, if we do not, then we are entitled to treat them as we like, imprisoning them, killing them, dishonoring their corpses.) I return to the death camps. The particular horror of the camps, the horror that convinces us that what went on there was a crime against humanity, is not that despite a humanity shared with their victims, the killers treated them like lice. That is too abstract. The horror is that the killers refused to think themselves into the place of their victims, as did everyone else. They said, 'It is *they* in those cattle-cars rattling past.' They did not say, 'How would it be if it were I in that cattle-car?' They did not say, 'It is I who am in that cattle-car.' They said, 'It must be the dead who are being burnt today, making the air stink and falling in ash on my cabbages.' They did not say, 'How would it be if I were burning?' They did not say, 'I am burning, I am falling in ash.'

"In other words, they closed their hearts. The heart is the seat of a faculty, *sympathy*, that allows us to share at times the being of another. Sympathy has everything to do with the subject and little

[11] John Berger: "Nowhere in a zoo can a stranger encounter the look of an animal. At the most, the animal's gaze flickers and passes on. They look sideways. They look blindly beyond. They scan mechanically. . . . That look between animal and man, which may have played a crucial role in the development of human society, and with which, in any case, all men had always lived until less than a century ago, has been extinguished." *About Looking* (New York: Pantheon, 1980), 26.

to do with the object, the 'another,' as we see at once when we think of the object not as a bat ('Can I share the being of a bat?') but as another human being. There are people who have the capacity to imagine themselves as someone else, there are people who have no such capacity (when the lack is extreme, we call them psychopaths), and there are people who have the capacity but choose not to exercise it.

"Despite Thomas Nagel, who is probably a good man, despite Thomas Aquinas and René Descartes, with whom I have more difficulty in sympathizing, there is no limit to the extent to which we can think ourselves into the being of another. There are no bounds to the sympathetic imagination. If you want proof, consider the following. Some years ago I wrote a book called *The House on Eccles Street*. To write that book I had to think my way into the existence of Marion Bloom. Either I succeeded or I did not. If I did not, I cannot imagine why you invited me here today. In any event, the point is, *Marion Bloom never existed*. Marion Bloom was a figment of James Joyce's imagination. If I can think my way into the existence of a being who has never existed, then I can think my way into the existence of a bat or a chimpanzee or an oyster, any being with whom I share the substrate of life.

"I return one last time to the places of death all around us, the places of slaughter to which, in a huge communal effort, we close our hearts. Each day a fresh holocaust, yet, as far as I can see, our moral being is untouched. We do not feel tainted. We can do anything, it seems, and come away clean.

"We point to the Germans and Poles and Ukrainians who did and did not know of the atrocities around them. We like to think they were inwardly marked by the aftereffects of that special form of ignorance. We like to think that in their nightmares the ones whose suffering they had refused to enter came back to haunt them. We like to think they woke up haggard in the mornings and died of gnawing cancers. But probably it was not so. The evidence points in the opposite direction: that we can do anything and get away with it; that there is no punishment."

A strange ending. Only when she takes off her glasses and folds away her papers does the applause start, and even then it is scattered. A strange ending to a strange talk, he thinks, ill gauged, ill argued. Not her métier, argumentation. She should not be here.

Norma has her hand up, is trying to catch the eyes of the dean of humanities, who is chairing the session.

"Norma!" he whispers. Urgently he shakes his head. "No!"

"Why?" she whispers back.

"Please," he whispers: "not here, not now!"

"There will be an extended discussion of our eminent guest's lecture on Friday at noon—you will see the details in your program notes—but Ms. Costello has kindly agreed to take one or two questions from the floor. So—?" The dean looks around brightly. "Yes!" he says, recognizing someone behind them.

"I have a right!" whispers Norma into his ear.

"You have a right, just don't exercise it, it's not a good idea!" he whispers back.

"She can't just be allowed to get away with it! She's confused!"

"She's old, she's my mother. Please!"

Behind them someone is already speaking. He turns and sees a tall, bearded man. God knows, he thinks, why his mother ever agreed to field questions from the floor. She ought to know that public lectures draw kooks and crazies like flies to a corpse.

"What wasn't clear to me," the man is saying, "is what you are actually targeting. Are you saying we should close down the factory farms? Are you saying we should stop eating meat? Are you saying we should treat animals more humanely, kill them more humanely? Are you saying we should stop experiments *on* animals? Are you saying we should stop experiments *with* animals, even benign psychological experiments like Köhler's? Can you clarify? Thank you."

Clarify. Not a kook at all. His mother could do with some clarity.

Standing before the microphone without her text before her, gripping the edges of the rostrum, his mother looks distinctly nervous. Not her métier, he thinks again: she should not be doing this.

"I was hoping not to have to enunciate principles," his mother says. "If principles are what you want to take away from this talk, I would have to respond, open your heart and listen to what your heart says."

She seems to want to leave it there. The dean looks nonplussed. No doubt the questioner feels nonplussed too. He himself certainly does. Why can't she just come out and say what she wants to say?

As if recognizing the stir of dissatisfaction, his mother resumes. "I have never been much interested in proscriptions, dietary or otherwise. Proscriptions, laws. I am more interested in what lies behind them. As for Köhler's experiments, I think he wrote a wonderful book, and the book wouldn't have been written if he hadn't thought he was a scientist conducting experiments with chimpanzees. But the book we read isn't the book he thought he was writing. I am reminded of something Montaigne said: We think we are playing with the cat, but how do we know that the cat isn't playing with us?[12] I wish I could think the animals in our laboratories are playing with us. But alas, it isn't so."

She falls silent. "Does that answer your question?" asks the dean. The questioner gives a huge, expressive shrug and sits down.

There is still the dinner to get through. In half an hour the president is to host a dinner at the Faculty Club. Initially he and Norma had not been invited. Then, after it was discovered that Elizabeth Costello had a son at Appleton, they were added to the list. He suspects they will be out of place. They will certainly be the most junior, the lowliest. On the other hand, it may be a good thing for him to be present. He may be needed to keep the peace.

With grim interest he looks forward to seeing how the college will cope with the challenge of the menu. If today's distinguished

---

[12] "Apology for Raimon Sebonde."

lecturer were an Islamic cleric or a Jewish rabbi, they would presumably not serve pork. So are they, out of deference to vegetarianism, going to serve nut rissoles to everyone? Are her distinguished fellow guests going to have to fret through the evening, dreaming of the pastrami sandwich or the cold drumstick they will gobble down when they get home? Or will the wise minds of the college have recourse to the ambiguous fish, which has a backbone but does not breathe air or suckle its young?

The menu is, fortunately, not his responsibility. What he dreads is that, during a lull in the conversation, someone will come up with what he calls The Question—"What led you, Mrs. Costello, to become a vegetarian?"—and that she will then get on her high horse and produce what he and Norma call The Plutarch Response. After that it will be up to him and him alone to repair the damage.

The response in question comes from Plutarch's moral essays. His mother has it by heart; he can reproduce it only imperfectly. "You ask me why I refuse to eat flesh. I, for my part, am astonished that you can put in your mouth the corpse of a dead animal, astonished that you do not find it nasty to chew hacked flesh and swallow the juices of death-wounds."[13] Plutarch is a real conversation-stopper: it is the word *juices* that does it. Producing Plutarch is like throwing down a gauntlet; after that, there is no knowing what will happen.

He wishes his mother had not come. It is nice to see her again; it is nice that she should see her grandchildren; it is nice for her to get recognition; but the price he is paying and the price he stands to pay if the visit goes badly seem to him excessive. Why can she not be an ordinary old woman living an ordinary old woman's life? If she wants to open her heart to animals, why can't she stay home and open it to her cats?

His mother is seated at the middle of the table, opposite President Garrard. He is seated two places away; Norma is at the foot of the table. One place is empty—he wonders whose.

---

[13] Cf. Plutarch, "Of Eating of Flesh," in Regan and Singer, *Animal Rights*, 111.

Ruth Orkin, from Psychology, is telling his mother about an experiment with a young chimpanzee reared as human. Asked to sort photographs into piles, the chimpanzee insisted on putting a picture of herself with the pictures of humans rather than with the pictures of other apes. "One is so tempted to give the story a straightforward reading," says Orkin—"namely, that she wanted to be thought of as one of us. Yet as a scientist one has to be cautious."

"Oh, I agree," says his mother. "In her mind the two piles could have a less obvious meaning. Those who are free to come and go versus those who have to stay locked up, for instance. She may have been saying that she preferred to be among the free."

"Or she may just have wanted to please her keeper," interjects President Garrard. "By saying that they looked alike."

"A bit Machiavellian for an animal, don't you think?" says a large blond man whose name he did not catch.

"Machiavelli the fox, his contemporaries called him," says his mother.

"But that's a different matter entirely—the fabulous qualities of animals," objects the large man.

"Yes," says his mother.

It is all going smoothly enough. They have been served pumpkin soup and no one is complaining. Can he afford to relax?

He was right about the fish. For the entree the choice is between red snapper with baby potatoes and fettucine with roasted eggplant. Garrard orders the fettucine, as he does; in fact, among the eleven of them there are only three fish orders.

"Interesting how often religious communities choose to define themselves in terms of dietary prohibitions," observes Garrard.

"Yes," says his mother.

"I mean, it is interesting that the form of the definition should be, for instance, 'We are the people who don't eat snakes' rather than 'We are the people who eat lizards.' What we don't do rather than what we do do." Before his move into administration, Garrard was a political scientist.

"It all has to do with cleanness and uncleanness," says Wunderlich, who despite his name is British. "Clean and unclean animals, clean and unclean habits. Uncleanness can be a very handy device for deciding who belongs and who doesn't, who is in and who is out."

"Uncleanness and shame," he himself interjects. "Animals have no shame." He is surprised to hear himself speaking. But why not?—the evening is going well.

"Exactly," says Wunderlich. "Animals don't hide their excretions, they perform sex in the open. They have no sense of shame, we say: that is what makes them different from us. But the basic idea remains uncleanness. Animals have unclean habits, so they are excluded. Shame makes human beings of us, shame of uncleanness. Adam and Eve: the founding myth. Before that we were all just animals together."

He has never heard Wunderlich before. He likes him, likes his earnest, stuttering, Oxford manner. A relief from American self-confidence.

"But that can't be how the mechanism works," objects Olivia Garrard, the president's elegant wife. "It's too abstract, too much of a bloodless idea. Animals are creatures we don't have sex with—that's how we distinguish them from ourselves. The very thought of sex with them makes us shudder. That is the level at which they are unclean—all of them. We don't mix with them. We keep the clean apart from the unclean."

"But we eat them." The voice is Norma's. "We do mix with them. We ingest them. We turn their flesh into ours. So it can't be how the mechanism works. There are specific kinds of animal that we don't eat. Surely *those* are the unclean ones, not animals in general."

She is right, of course. But wrong: a mistake to bring the conversation back to the matter on the table before them, the food.

Wunderlich speaks again. "The Greeks had a feeling there was something wrong in slaughter, but thought they could make up for that by ritualizing it. They made a sacrificial offering, gave a percentage to the gods, hoping thereby to keep the rest. The same notion as the tithe. Ask for the blessing of the gods on the flesh you are about to eat, ask them to declare it clean."

"Perhaps that is the origin of the gods," says his mother. A silence falls. "Perhaps we invented gods so that we could put the blame on them. They gave us permission to eat flesh. They gave us permission to play with unclean things. It's not our fault, it's theirs. We're just their children."[14]

"Is that what you believe?" asks Mrs. Garrard cautiously.

"And God said: Every moving thing that liveth shall be meat for you," his mother quotes. "It's convenient. God told us it was OK."

Silence again. They are waiting for her to go on. She is, after all, the paid entertainer.

"Norma is right," says his mother. "The problem is to define our difference from animals in general, not just from so-called unclean animals. The ban on certain animals—pigs and so forth—is quite arbitrary. It is simply a signal that we are in a danger area. A minefield, in fact. The minefield of dietary proscriptions. There is no logic to a taboo, nor is there any logic to a minefield—there is not meant to be. You can never guess what you may eat or where you may step unless you are in possession of a map, a divine map."

"But that's just anthropology," objects Norma from the foot of the table. "It says nothing about our behavior today. People in the modern world no longer decide their diet on the basis of whether they have divine permission. If we eat pig and don't eat dog, that's just the way we are brought up. Wouldn't you agree, Elizabeth? It's just one of our folkways."

---

[14] James Serpell, quoting Walter Burkert, *Homo necans*, describes the ritual of animal sacrifice in the ancient world as "an elaborate exercise in blame-shifting." The animal delivered to the temple was by various means made to seem to assent to its death, while the priests took precautions to cleanse themselves of guilt. "It was ultimately the gods who were to blame, since it was they who demanded the sacrifice." In Greece the Pythagoreans and Orphics condemned these sacrifices "precisely because the underlying carnivorous motives were so obvious." *In the Company of Animals* (Oxford: Blackwell, 1986), 167–68.

Elizabeth. She is claiming intimacy. But what game is she playing? Is there a trap she is leading his mother into?

"There is disgust," says his mother. "We may have got rid of the gods but we have not got rid of disgust, which is a version of religious horror."

"Disgust is not universal," objects Norma. "The French eat frogs. The Chinese eat anything. There is no disgust in China."

His mother is silent.

"So perhaps it's just a matter of what you learned at home, of what your mother told you was OK to eat and what was not."

"What was clean to eat and what was not," his mother murmurs.

"And maybe"—now Norma is going too far, he thinks, now she is beginning to dominate the conversation to an extent that is totally inappropriate—"the whole notion of cleanness versus uncleanness has a completely different function, namely, to enable certain groups to self-define themselves, negatively, as elite, as elected. We are the people who abstain from *a* or *b* or *c*, and by that power of abstinence we mark ourselves off as superior: as a superior caste within society, for instance. Like the Brahmins."

There is a silence.

"The ban on meat that you get in vegetarianism is only an extreme form of dietary ban," Norma presses on; "and a dietary ban is a quick, simple way for an elite group to define itself. Other people's table habits are unclean, we can't eat or drink with them."

Now she is getting really close to the bone. There is a certain amount of shuffling, there is unease in the air. Fortunately the course is over—the red snapper, the tagliatelle—and the waitresses are among them removing the plates.

"Have you read Gandhi's autobiography, Norma?" asks his mother.

"No."

"Gandhi was sent off to England as a young man to study law. England, of course, prided itself as a great meat-eating country.

But his mother made him promise not to eat meat. She packed a trunk full of food for him to take along. During the sea voyage he scavenged a little bread from the ship's table and for the rest ate out of his trunk. In London he faced a long search for lodgings and eating-houses that served his kind of food. Social relations with the English were difficult because he could not accept or return hospitality. It wasn't until he fell in with certain fringe elements of English society—Fabians, theosophists, and so forth—that he began to feel at home. Until then he was just a lonely little law student."

"What is the point, Elizabeth?" says Norma. "What is the point of the story?"

"Just that Gandhi's vegetarianism can hardly be conceived as the exercise of power. It condemned him to the margins of society. It was his particular genius to incorporate what he found on those margins into his political philosophy."

"In any event," interjects the blond man, "Gandhi is not a good example. His vegetarianism was hardly committed. He was a vegetarian because of the promise he made to his mother. He may have kept his promise, but he regretted and resented it."

"Don't you think that mothers can have a good influence on their children?" says Elizabeth Costello.

There is a moment's silence. It is time for him, the good son, to speak. He does not.

"But your own vegetarianism, Mrs. Costello," says President Garrard, pouring oil on troubled waters: "it comes out of moral conviction, does it not?"

"No, I don't think so," says his mother. "It comes out of a desire to save my soul."

Now there truly is a silence, broken only by the clink of plates as the waitresses set baked Alaskas before them.

"Well, I have a great respect for it," says Garrard. "As a way of life."

"I'm wearing leather shoes," says his mother. "I'm carrying a leather purse. I wouldn't have overmuch respect if I were you."

"Consistency," murmurs Garrard. "Consistency is the hobgoblin of small minds. Surely one can draw a distinction between eating meat and wearing leather."

"Degrees of obscenity," she replies.

"I too have the greatest respect for codes based on respect for life," says Dean Arendt, entering the debate for the first time. "I am prepared to accept that dietary taboos do not have to be mere customs. I will accept that underlying them are genuine moral concerns. But at the same time one must say that our whole superstructure of concern and belief is a closed book to animals themselves. You can't explain to a steer that its life is going to be spared, any more than you can explain to a bug that you are not going to step on it. In the lives of animals, things, good or bad, just happen. So vegetarianism is a very odd transaction, when you come to think of it, with the beneficiaries unaware that they are being benefited. And with no hope of ever becoming aware. Because they live in a vacuum of consciousness."

Arendt pauses. It is his mother's turn to speak, but she merely looks confused, gray and tired and confused. He leans across. "It's been a long day, mother," he says. "Perhaps it is time."

"Yes, it is time," she says.

"You won't have coffee?" inquires President Garrard.

"No, it will just keep me awake." She turns to Arendt. "That is a good point you raise. No consciousness that we would recognize as consciousness. No awareness, as far as we can make out, of a self with a history. What I mind is what tends to come next. They have no consciousness *therefore*. Therefore what? Therefore we are free to use them for our own ends? Therefore we are free to kill them? Why? What is so special about the form of consciousness we recognize that makes killing a bearer of it a crime while killing an animal goes unpunished? There are moments—"

"To say nothing of babies," interjects Wunderlich. Everyone turns and looks at him. "Babies have no self-consciousness, yet we think it a more heinous crime to kill a baby than an adult."

"Therefore?" says Arendt.

"Therefore all this discussion of consciousness and whether animals have it is just a smoke screen. At bottom we protect our own kind. Thumbs up to human babies, thumbs down to veal calves. Don't you think so, Mrs. Costello?"

"I don't know what I think," says Elizabeth Costello. "I often wonder what thinking is, what understanding is. Do we really understand the universe better than animals do? Understanding a thing often looks to me like playing with one of those Rubik cubes. Once you have made all the little bricks snap into place, hey presto, you understand. It makes sense if you live inside a Rubik cube, but if you don't . . ."

There is a silence. "I would have thought—" says Norma; but at this point he gets to his feet, and to his relief Norma stops.

The president rises, and then everyone else. "A wonderful lecture, Mrs. Costello," says the president. "Much food for thought. We look forward to tomorrow's offering."

The Poets and the Animals

❖

IT IS AFTER ELEVEN. His mother has retired for the night, he and Norma are downstairs clearing up the children's mess. After that he still has a class to prepare.

"Are you going to her seminar tomorrow?" asks Norma.

"I'll have to."

"What is it on?"

"'The Poets and the Animals.' That's the title. The English Department is staging it. They are holding it in a seminar room, so I don't think they are expecting a big audience."

"I'm glad it's on something she knows about. I find her philosophizing rather difficult to take."

"Oh. What do you have in mind?"

"For instance what she was saying about human reason. Presumably she was trying to make a point about the nature of rational understanding. To say that rational accounts are merely a consequence of the structure of the human mind; that animals have their own accounts in accordance with the structure of their own minds, to which we don't have access because we don't share a language with them."

"And what's wrong with that?"

"It's naive, John. It's the kind of easy, shallow relativism that impresses freshmen. Respect for everyone's worldview, the cow's worldview, the squirrel's worldview, and so forth. In the end it leads to total intellectual paralysis. You spend so much time respecting that you haven't time left to think."

"Doesn't a squirrel have a worldview?"

47

"Yes, a squirrel does have a worldview. Its worldview comprises acorns and trees and weather and cats and dogs and automobiles and squirrels of the opposite sex. It comprises an account of how these phenomena interact and how it should interact with them to survive. That's all. There's no more. That's the world according to squirrel."

"We are sure about that?"

"We are sure about it in the sense that hundreds of years of observing squirrels has not led us to conclude otherwise. If there is anything else in the squirrel mind, it does not issue in observable behavior. For all practical purposes, the mind of the squirrel is a very simple mechanism."

"So Descartes was right, animals are just biological automata."

"Broadly speaking, yes. You cannot, in the abstract, distinguish between an animal mind and a machine simulating an animal mind."

"And human beings are different?"

"John, I am tired and you are being irritating. Human beings invent mathematics, they build telescopes, they do calculations, they construct machines, they press a button, and, bang, *Sojourner* lands on Mars, exactly as predicted. That is why rationality is not just, as your mother claims, a game. Reason provides us with real knowledge of the real world. It has been tested, and it works. You are a physicist. You ought to know."

"I agree. It works. Still, isn't there a position outside from which our doing our thinking and then sending out a Mars probe looks a lot like a squirrel doing its thinking and then dashing out and snatching a nut? Isn't that perhaps what she meant?"

"But there isn't any such position! I know it sounds old-fashioned, but I have to say it. There is no position outside of reason where you can stand and lecture about reason and pass judgment on reason."

"Except the position of someone who has withdrawn from reason."

"That's just French irrationalism, the sort of thing a person would say who has never set foot inside a mental institution and seen what people look like who have *really* withdrawn from reason."

"Then except for God."

"Not if God is a God of reason. A God of reason cannot stand outside reason."

"I'm surprised, Norma. You are talking like an old-fashioned rationalist."

"You misunderstand me. That is the ground your mother has chosen. Those are her terms. I am merely responding."

"Who was the missing guest?"

"You mean the empty seat? It was Stern, the poet."

"Do you think it was a protest?"

"I'm sure it was. She should have thought twice before bringing up the Holocaust. I could feel hackles rising all around me in the audience."

The empty seat was indeed a protest. When he goes in for his morning class, there is a letter in his box addressed to his mother. He hands it over to her when he comes home to fetch her. She reads it quickly, then with a sigh passes it over to him. "Who is this man?" she says.

"Abraham Stern. A poet. Quite well-respected, I believe. He has been here donkey's years."

He reads Stern's note, which is handwritten.

Dear Mrs. Costello,

Excuse me for not attending last night's dinner. I have read your books and know you are a serious person, so I do you the credit of taking what you said in your lecture seriously.

At the kernel of your lecture, it seemed to me, was the question of breaking bread. If we refuse to break bread with the executioners of Auschwitz, can we continue to break bread with the slaughterers of animals?

You took over for your own purposes the familiar comparison between the murdered Jews of Europe and slaughtered cattle. The Jews died like cattle, therefore cattle die like Jews, you say. That is a trick with words which I will not accept. You misunderstand the nature of likenesses; I would even say you misunderstand willfully, to the point of blasphemy. Man is made in the likeness of God but God does not have the likeness of man. If Jews were treated like cattle, it does not follow that cattle are treated like Jews. The inversion insults the memory of the dead. It also trades on the horrors of the camps in a cheap way.

Forgive me if I am forthright. You said you were old enough not to have time to waste on niceties, and I am an old man too.

Yours sincerely,
Abraham Stern.

HE delivers his mother to her hosts in the English Department, then goes to a meeting. The meeting drags on and on. It is two-thirty before he can get to the seminar room in Stubbs Hall.

She is speaking as he enters. He sits down as quietly as he can near the door.

"In that kind of poetry," she is saying, "animals stand for human qualities: the lion for courage, the owl for wisdom, and so forth. Even in Rilke's poem the panther is there as a stand-in for something else. He dissolves into a dance of energy around a center, an image that comes from physics, elementary particle physics. Rilke does not get beyond this point—beyond the panther as the vital embodiment of the kind of force that is released in an atomic explosion but is here trapped not so much by the bars of the cage as by what the bars compel on the panther: a concentric lope that leaves the will stupefied, narcotized."

Rilke's panther? What panther? His confusion must show: the girl next to him pushes a photocopied sheet under his nose. Three poems: one by Rilke called "The Panther," two by Ted Hughes called "The Jaguar" and "Second Glance at a Jaguar." He has no time to read them.

"Hughes is writing against Rilke," his mother goes on. "He uses the same staging in the zoo, but it is the crowd for a change that stands mesmerized, and among them the man, the poet, entranced and horrified and overwhelmed, his powers of under-

standing pushed beyond their limit. The jaguar's vision, unlike
the panther's, is not blunted. On the contrary, his eyes drill
through the darkness of space. The cage has no reality to him, he
is *elsewhere*. He is elsewhere because his consciousness is kinetic
rather than abstract: the thrust of his muscles moves him through
a space quite different in nature from the three-dimensional box
of Newton—a circular space that returns upon itself.

"So—leaving aside the ethics of caging large animals—Hughes
is feeling his way toward a different kind of being-in-the-world,
one which is not entirely foreign to us, since the experience before the cage seems to belong to dream-experience, experience
held in the collective unconscious. In these poems we know the
jaguar not from the way he seems but from the way he moves.
The body is as the body moves, or as the currents of life move
within it. The poems ask us to imagine our way into that way of
moving, to inhabit that body.

"With Hughes it is a matter—I emphasize—not of inhabiting
another mind but of inhabiting another body. That is the kind of
poetry I bring to your attention today: poetry that does not try to
find an idea in the animal, that is not about the animal, but is
instead the record of an engagement with him.

"What is peculiar about poetic engagements of this kind is that,
no matter with what intensity they take place, they remain a matter of complete indifference to their objects. In this respect they
are different from love poems, where your intention is to move
your object.

"Not that animals do not care what we feel about them. But
when we divert the current of feeling that flows between ourself
and the animal into words, we abstract it forever from the animal.
Thus the poem is not a gift to its object, as the love poem is. It
falls within an entirely human economy in which the animal has
no share. Does that answer your question?"

Someone else has his hand up: a tall young man with glasses.
He doesn't know Ted Hughes's poetry well, he says, but the last
he heard, Hughes was running a sheep ranch somewhere in

England. Either he is just raising sheep as poetic subjects (there is a titter around the room) or he is a real rancher raising sheep for the market. "How does this square with what you were saying in your lecture yesterday, when you seemed to be pretty much against killing animals for meat?"

"I've never met Ted Hughes," replies his mother, "so I can't tell you what kind of farmer he is. But let me try to answer your question on another level.

"I have no reason to think that Hughes believes his attentiveness to animals is unique. On the contrary, I suspect he believes he is recovering an attentiveness that our faraway ancestors possessed and we have lost (he conceives of this loss in evolutionary rather than historical terms, but that is another question). I would guess that he believes he looks at animals much as paleolithic hunters used to.

"This puts Hughes in a line of poets who celebrate the primitive and repudiate the Western bias toward abstract thought. The line of Blake and Lawrence, of Gary Snyder in the United States, or Robinson Jeffers. Hemingway too, in his hunting and bull-fighting phase.

"Bullfighting, it seems to me, gives us a clue. Kill the beast by all means, they say, but make it a contest, a ritual, and honor your antagonist for his strength and bravery. Eat him too, after you have vanquished him, in order for his strength and courage to enter you. Look him in the eyes before you kill him, and thank him afterwards. Sing songs about him.

"We can call this primitivism. It is an attitude that is easy to criticize, to mock. It is deeply masculine, masculinist. Its ramifications into politics are to be mistrusted. But when all is said and done, there remains something attractive about it at an ethical level.

"It is also impractical, however. You do not feed four billion people through the efforts of matadors or deer-hunters armed with bows and arrows. We have become too many. There is no time to respect and honor all the animals we need to feed ourselves. We need factories of death; we need factory animals. Chicago showed us the way; it was from the Chicago stockyards that the Nazis learned how to process bodies.

"But let me get back to Hughes. You say: Despite the primitivist trappings Hughes is a butcher, and what am I doing in his company?

"I would reply, writers teach us more than they are aware of. By bodying forth the jaguar, Hughes shows us that we too can embody animals—by the process called poetic invention that mingles breath and sense in a way that no one has explained and no one ever will. He shows us how to bring the living body into being within ourselves. When we read the jaguar poem, when we recollect it afterwards in tranquillity, we are for a brief while the jaguar. He ripples within us, he takes over our body, he is us.

"So far, so good. With what I have said thus far I don't think Hughes himself would disagree. It is much like the mixture of shamanism and spirit possession and archetype psychology that he himself espouses. In other words, a primitive experience (being face to face with an animal), a primitivist poem, and a primitivist theory of poetry to justify it.

"It is also the kind of poetry with which hunters and the people I call ecology-managers can feel comfortable. When Hughes the poet stands before the jaguar cage, he looks at an individual jaguar and is possessed by that individual jaguar life. It has to be that way. Jaguars in general, the subspecies jaguar, the idea of a jaguar, will fail to move him because we cannot experience abstractions. Nevertheless, the poem that Hughes writes is about *the* jaguar, about jaguarness embodied in this jaguar. Just as later on, when he writes his marvelous poems about salmon, they are about salmon as transitory occupants of the salmon-life, the salmon-biography. So despite the vividness and earthiness of the poetry, there remains something Platonic about it.

"In the ecological vision, the salmon and the river-weeds and the water-insects interact in a great, complex dance with the earth and the weather. The whole is greater than the sum of the parts.

In the dance, each organism has a role: it is these multiple roles, rather than the particular beings who play them, that participate in the dance. As for actual role-players, as long as they are self-renewing, as long as they keep coming forward, we need pay them no heed.

"I called this Platonic and I do so again. Our eye is on the creature itself, but our mind is on the system of interactions of which it is the earthly, material embodiment.

"The irony is a terrible one. An ecological philosophy that tells us to live side by side with other creatures justifies itself by appealing to an idea, an idea of a higher order than any living creature. An idea, finally—and this is the crushing twist to the irony—which no creature except Man is capable of comprehending. Every living creature fights for its own, individual life, refuses, by fighting, to accede to the idea that the salmon or the gnat is of a lower order of importance than the idea of the salmon or the idea of the gnat. But when we see the salmon fighting for its life, we say, it is just programmed to fight; we say, with Aquinas, it is locked into natural slavery; we say, it lacks self-consciousness.

"Animals are not believers in ecology. Even the ethnobiologists do not make that claim. Even the ethnobiologists do not say that the ant sacrifices its life to perpetuate the species. What they say is subtly different: the ant dies and the function of its death is the perpetuation of the species. The species-life is a force which acts through the individual but which the individual is incapable of understanding. In that sense the idea is innate, and the ant is run by the idea as a computer is run by a program.

"We, the managers of the ecology—I'm sorry to go on like this, I am getting way beyond your question, I'll be through in a moment—we managers understand the greater dance, therefore we can decide how many trout may be fished or how many jaguar may be trapped before the stability of the dance is upset. The only organism over which we do not claim this power of life and death is Man. Why? Because Man is different. Man understands the dance as the other dancers do not. Man is an intellectual being."

While she speaks, his mind has been wandering. He has heard it before, this antiecologism of hers. Jaguar poems are all very well, he thinks, but you won't get a bunch of Australians standing around a sheep, listening to its silly baa, writing poems about it. Isn't that what is so suspect in the whole animals-rights business: that it has to ride on the back of pensive gorillas and sexy jaguars and huggable pandas because the real objects of its concern, chickens and pigs, to say nothing of white rats or prawns, are not newsworthy?

Now Elaine Marx, who did the introduction to yesterday's lecture, asks a question. "In your lecture you argued that various criteria—Does this creature have reason? Does this creature have speech?—have been used in bad faith to justify distinctions that have no real basis, between *Homo* and other primates, for example, and thus to justify exploitation.

"Yet the very fact that you can be arguing against this reasoning, exposing its falsity, means that you put a certain faith in the power of reason, of true reason as opposed to false reason.

"Let me concretize my question by referring to the case of Lemuel Gulliver. In *Gulliver's Travels* Swift gives us a vision of a utopia of reason, the land of the so-called Houyhnhnms, but it turns out to be a place where there is no home for Gulliver, who is the closest that Swift comes to a representation of us, his readers. But which of us would want to live in Houyhnhnm-land, with its rational vegetarianism and its rational government and its rational approach to love, marriage, and death? Would even a horse want to live in such a perfectly regulated, totalitarian society? More pertinently for us, what is the track record of totally regulated societies? Is it not a fact that they either collapse or else turn militaristic?

"Specifically, my question is: Are you not expecting too much of humankind when you ask us to live without species exploitation, without cruelty? Is it not more human to accept our own humanity—even if it means embracing the carnivorous Yahoo within ourselves—than to end up like Gulliver, pining for a state he can never attain, and for good reason: it is not in his nature, which is a human nature?'

"An interesting question," his mother replies. "I find Swift an intriguing writer. For instance, his 'Modest Proposal.' Whenever there is overwhelming agreement about how to read a book, I prick up my ears. On 'A Modest Proposal' the consensus is that Swift does not mean what he says, or seems to say. He says, or seems to say, that Irish families could make a living by raising babies for the table of their English masters. But he can't mean that, we say, because we all know that it is atrocious to kill and eat human babies. Yet, come to think of it, we go on, the English are already in a sense killing human babies, by letting them starve. So, come to think of it, the English are already atrocious.

"That is the orthodox reading, more or less. But why, I ask myself, the vehemence with which it is stuffed down the throats of young readers? Thus shall you read Swift, their teachers say, thus and in no other way. If it is atrocious to kill and eat human babies, why is it not atrocious to kill and eat piglets? If you want Swift to be a dark ironist rather than a facile pamphleteer, you might examine the premises that make his fable so easy to digest.

"Let me now turn to *Gulliver's Travels*.

"On the one hand you have the Yahoos, who are associated with raw meat, the smell of excrement, and what we used to call bestiality. On the other you have the Houyhnhnms, who are associated with grass, sweet smells, and the rational ordering of the passions. In between you have Gulliver, who wants to be a Houyhnhnm but knows secretly that he is a Yahoo. All of that is perfectly clear. As with 'A Modest Proposal,' the question is, what do we make of it?

"One observation. The horses expel Gulliver. Their ostensible reason is that he does not meet the standard of rationality. The real reason is that he does not look like a horse, but something else: a dressed-up Yahoo, in fact. So: the standard of reason that has been applied by carnivorous bipeds to justify a special status for themselves can equally be applied by herbivorous quadrupeds.

"The standard of reason. *Gulliver's Travels* seems to me to operate within the three-part Aristotelian division of gods, beasts, and men. As long as one tries to fit the three actors into just two categories—which are the beasts, which are the men?—one can't make sense of the fable. Nor can the Houyhnhnms. The Houyhnhnms are gods of a kind, cold, Apollonian. The test they apply to Gulliver is: Is he a god or a beast? They feel it is the appropriate test. We, instinctively, don't.

"What has always puzzled me about *Gulliver's Travels*—and this is a perspective you might expect from an ex-colonial—is that Gulliver always travels alone. Gulliver goes on voyages of exploration to unknown lands, but he does not come ashore with an armed party, *as happened in reality*, and Swift's book says nothing about what would normally have come after Gulliver's pioneering efforts: follow-up expeditions, expeditions to colonize Lilliput or the island of the Houyhnhnms.

"The question I ask is: What if Gulliver and an armed expedition were to land, shoot a few Yahoos when they become threatening, and then shoot and eat a horse, for food? What would that do to Swift's somewhat too neat, somewhat too disembodied, somewhat too unhistorical fable? It would certainly give the Houyhnhnms a rude shock, making it clear that there is a third category besides gods and beasts, namely, man, of whom their ex-client Gulliver is one; furthermore, that if the horses stand for reason, then man stands for physical force.

"Taking over an island and slaughtering its inhabitants is, by the way, what Odysseus and his men did on Thrinacia, the island sacred to Apollo, an act for which they were mercilessly punished by the god. And that story, in turn, seems to call on older layers of belief, from a time when bulls were gods and killing and eating a god could call down a curse on you.

"So—excuse the confusion of this response—yes, we are not horses, we do not have their clear, rational, naked beauty; on the contrary, we are subequine primates, otherwise known as man. You say there is nothing to do but embrace that status, that nature. Very well, let us do so. But let us also push Swift's fable to its limits and recognize that, in history, embracing the status of man has entailed slaughtering and enslaving a race of divine or else divinely created beings and bringing down on ourselves a curse thereby."

Iᴛ ɪs three-fifteen, a couple of hours before his mother's last engagement. He walks her over to his office along tree-lined paths where the last autumn leaves are falling.

"Do you really believe, Mother, that poetry classes are going to close down the slaughterhouses?"

"No."

"Then why do it? You said you were tired of clever talk about animals, proving by syllogism that they do or do not have souls. But isn't poetry just another kind of clever talk: admiring the muscles of the big cats in verse? Wasn't your point about talk that it changes nothing? It seems to me the level of behavior you want to change is too elementary, too elemental, to be reached by talk. Carnivorousness expresses something truly deep about human beings, just as it does about jaguars. You wouldn't want to put a jaguar on a soybean diet."

"Because he would die. Human beings don't die on a vegetarian diet."

"No, they don't. But they don't *want* a vegetarian diet. They *like* eating meat. There is something atavistically satisfying about it. That's the brutal truth. Just as it's a brutal truth that, in a sense, animals deserve what they get. Why waste your time trying to help them when they won't help themselves? Let them stew in their own juice. If I were asked what the general attitude is toward the animals we eat, I would say: contempt. We treat them badly because we despise them; we despise them because they don't fight back."

"I don't disagree," says his mother. "People complain that we treat animals like objects, but in fact we treat them like prisoners of war. Do you know that when zoos were first opened to the public, the keepers had to protect the animals against attacks by spectators? The spectators felt the animals were there to be insulted and abused, like prisoners in a triumph. We had a war once against the animals, which we called hunting, though in fact war and hunting are the same thing (Aristotle saw it clearly).[1] That war went on for millions of years. We won it definitively only a few hundred years ago, when we invented guns. It is only since victory became absolute that we have been able to afford to cultivate compassion. But our compassion is very thinly spread. Beneath it is a more primitive attitude. The prisoner of war does not belong to our tribe. We can do what we want with him. We can sacrifice him to our gods. We can cut his throat, tear out his heart, throw him on the fire. There are no laws when it comes to prisoners of war."

"And that is what you want to cure humankind of?"

"John, I don't know what I want to do. I just don't want to sit silent."

"Very well. But generally one doesn't kill prisoners of war. One turns them into slaves."

"Well, that's what our captive herds are: slave populations. Their work is to breed for us. Even their sex becomes a form of labor. We don't hate them because they are not worth hating any more. We regard them, as you say, with contempt.

"However, there are still animals we hate. Rats, for instance. Rats haven't surrendered. They fight back. They form themselves into underground units in our sewers. They aren't winning, but they aren't losing either. To say nothing of the insects and the microbia. They may beat us yet. They will certainly outlast us."

THE final session of his mother's visit is to take the form of a debate. Her opponent will be the large, blond man from yesterday evening's dinner, who turns out to be Thomas O'Hearne, professor of philosophy at Appleton.

[1] Aristotle: "The art of war is a natural art of acquisition, for the art of acquisition includes hunting, an art which we ought to practise against wild beasts, and against men who, though intended by nature to be governed, will not submit; for war of such a kind is naturally just." *Politics* 1.8, in Regan and Singer, *Animal Rights*, 110.

It has been agreed that O'Hearne will have three opportunities to present positions, and his mother three opportunities to reply. Since O'Hearne has had the courtesy to send her a précis beforehand, she knows, broadly speaking, what he will be saying.

"My first reservation about the animal-rights movement," O'Hearne begins, "is that by failing to recognize its historical nature, it runs the risk of becoming, like the human-rights movement, yet another Western crusade against the practices of the rest of the world, claiming universality for what are simply its own standards." He proceeds to give a brief outline of the rise of animal-protection societies in Britain and America in the nineteenth century.

"When it comes to human rights," he continues, "other cultures and other religious traditions quite properly reply that they have their own norms and see no reason why they should have to adopt those of the West. Similarly, they say, they have their own norms for the treatment of animals and see no reason to adopt ours—particularly when ours are of such recent invention.

"In yesterday's presentation our lecturer was very hard on Descartes. But Descartes did not invent the idea that animals belong to a different order from humankind: he merely formalized it in a new way. The notion that we have an obligation to animals themselves to treat them compassionately—as opposed to an obligation to ourselves to do so—is very recent, very Western, and even very Anglo-Saxon. As long as we insist that we have access to an ethical universal to which other traditions are blind, and try to impose it on them by means of propaganda or even economic pressure, we are going to meet with resistance, and that resistance will be justified."

It is his mother's turn.

"The concerns you express are substantial, Professor O'Hearne, and I am not sure I can give them a substantial answer. You are correct, of course, about the history. Kindness to animals has become a social norm only recently, in the last hundred and fifty or two hundred years, and in only part of the world.

You are correct too to link this history to the history of human rights, since concern for animals is, historically speaking, an offshoot of broader philanthropic concerns—for the lot of slaves and of children, among others.[2]

"However, kindness to animals—and here I use the word *kindness* in its full sense, as an acceptance that we are all of one kind, one nature—has been more widespread than you imply. Pet keeping, for instance, is by no means a Western fad: the first travelers to South America encountered settlements where human beings and animals lived higgledy-piggledy together. And of course children all over the world consort quite naturally with animals. They don't see any dividing line. That is something they have to be taught, just as they have to be taught it is all right to kill and eat them.

"Getting back to Descartes, I would only want to say that the discontinuity he saw between animals and human beings was the result of incomplete information. The science of Descartes's day had no acquaintance with the great apes or with higher marine mammals, and thus little cause to question the assumption that animals cannot think. And of course it had no access to the fossil record that would reveal a graded continuum of anthropoid creatures stretching from the higher primates to *Homo sapiens*—anthropoids, one must point out, who were exterminated by man in the course of his rise to power.[3]

"While I concede your main point about Western cultural arrogance, I do think it is appropriate that those who pioneered the industrialization of animal lives and the commodification of animal flesh should be at the forefront of trying to atone for it."

O'Hearne presents his second thesis. "In my reading of the scientific literature," he says, "efforts to show that animals can

---

[2] See James Turner, *Reckoning with the Beast* (Baltimore: Johns Hopkins University Press, 1980), chap. 1.

[3] See Mary Midgley, "Persons and Non-Persons," in *In Defence of Animals*, ed. Peter Singer (Oxford: Blackwell, 1985), 59; Rosemary Rodd, *Biology, Ethics, and Animals* (Oxford: Clarendon Press, 1990), 37.

think strategically, hold general concepts, or communicate symbolically, have had very limited success. The best performance the higher apes can put up is no better than that of a speech-impaired human being with severe mental retardation. If so, are not animals, even the higher animals, properly thought of as belonging to another legal and ethical realm entirely, rather than being placed in this depressing human subcategory? Isn't there a certain wisdom in the traditional view that says that animals cannot enjoy legal rights because they are not persons, even potential persons, as fetuses are? In working out rules for our dealings with animals, does it not make more sense for such rules to apply to us and to our treatment of them, as at present, rather than being predicated upon rights which animals cannot claim or enforce or even understand?"[4]

His mother's turn. "To respond adequately, Professor O'Hearne, would take more time than I have, since I would first want to interrogate the whole question of rights and how we come to possess them. So let me just make one observation: that the program of scientific experimentation that leads you to conclude that animals are imbeciles is profoundly anthropocentric. It values being able to find your way out of a sterile maze, ignoring the fact that if the researcher who designed the maze were to be parachuted into the jungles of Borneo, he or she would be dead of starvation in a week. In fact I would go further. If I as a human being were told that the standards by which animals are being measured in these experiments are human standards, I would be insulted. It is the experiments themselves that are imbecile. The behaviorists who design them claim that we understand only by a process of creating abstract models and then testing those models against reality. What nonsense. We understand by immersing ourselves and our intelligence in complexity. There is something

---

[4] Cf. Bernard Williams: "Before one gets to the question of how animals should be treated, there is the fundamental point that this is the only question there can be: how they should be treated. The choice can only be whether animals benefit from our practices or are harmed by them." Quoted in Michael P. T. Leahy, *Against Liberation* (London and New York: Routledge, 1991), 208.

self-stultified in the way in which scientific behaviorism recoils from the complexity of life.[5]

"As for animals being too dumb and stupid to speak for themselves, consider the following sequence of events. When Albert Camus was a young boy in Algeria, his grandmother told him to bring her one of the hens from the cage in their backyard. He obeyed, then watched her cut off its head with a kitchen knife, catching its blood in a bowl so that the floor would not be dirtied.

"The death-cry of that hen imprinted itself on the boy's memory so hauntingly that in 1958 he wrote an impassioned attack on the guillotine. As a result, in part, of that polemic, capital punishment was abolished in France. Who is to say, then, that the hen did not speak?"[6]

O'Hearne. "I make the following statement with due deliberation, mindful of the historical associations it may evoke. I do not believe that life is as important to animals as it is to us. There is certainly in animals an instinctive struggle against death, which they share with us. But they do not *understand* death as we do, or rather, as we fail to do. There is, in the human mind, a collapse of the imagination before death, and that collapse of the imagination—graphically evoked in yesterday's lecture—is the basis of our fear of death. That fear does not and cannot exist in animals, since the effort to comprehend extinction, and the failure to do so, the failure to master it, have simply not taken place.

"For that reason, I want to suggest, dying is, for an animal, just something that happens, something against which there may be a revolt of the organism but not a revolt of the soul. And the lower

[5] For a critique of behaviorism in the political context of its times, see Bernard E. Rollin, *The Unheeded Cry* (Oxford: Oxford University Press, 1990), 100–103. On the behaviorist taboo on considering the subjective mental states of animals, see Donald R. Griffin, *Animal Minds* (Chicago: University of Chicago Press, 1992), 6–7. Griffin calls the taboo "a serious impediment to scientific investigation" but suggests that in practice investigators do not adhere to it (6, 120).

[6] Albert Camus, *The First Man*, trans. David Hapgood (London: Hamish Hamilton, 1995), 181–83; "Réflexions sur la guillotine," in *Essais*, ed. R. Quilliot and L. Faucon (Paris: Gallimard, 1965), 1019–64.

down the scale of evolution one goes, the truer this is. To an insect, death is the breakdown of systems that keep the physical organism functioning, and nothing more.

"To animals, death is continuous with life. It is only among certain very imaginative human beings that one encounters a horror of dying so acute that they then project it onto other beings, including animals. Animals live, and then they die: that is all. Thus to equate a butcher who slaughters a chicken with an executioner who kills a human being is a grave mistake. The events are not comparable. They are not of the same scale, they are not on the same scale.

"That leaves us with the question of cruelty. It is licit to kill animals, I would say, because their lives are not as important to them as our lives are to us; the old-fashioned way of saying this is that animals do not have immortal souls. Gratuitous cruelty, on the other hand, I would regard as illicit. Therefore it is quite appropriate that we should agitate for the humane treatment of animals, even and particularly in slaughterhouses. This has for a long time been a goal of animal welfare organizations, and I salute them for it.

"My very last point concerns what I see as the troublingly abstract nature of the concern for animals in the animal-rights movement. I want to apologize in advance to our lecturer for the seeming harshness of what I am about to say, but I believe it needs to be said.

"Of the many varieties of animal-lover I see around me, let me isolate two. On the one hand, hunters, people who value animals at a very elementary, unreflective level; who spend hours watching them and tracking them; and who, after they have killed them, get pleasure from the taste of their flesh. On the other hand, people who have little contact with animals, or at least with those species they are concerned to protect, like poultry and livestock, yet want all animals to lead—in an economic vacuum—a utopian life in which everyone is miraculously fed and no one preys on anyone else.

"Of the two, which, I ask, loves animals more?

"It is because agitation for animal rights, including the right to life, is so abstract that I find it unconvincing and, finally, idle. Its proponents talk a great deal about our community with animals, but how do they actually live that community? Thomas Aquinas says that friendship between human beings and animals is impossible, and I tend to agree.[7] You can be friends neither with a Martian nor with a bat, for the simple reason that you have too little in common with them. We may certainly *wish* for there to be community with animals, but that is not the same thing as living in community with them. It is just a piece of prelapsarian wistfulness."

His mother's turn again, her last turn.

"Anyone who says that life matters less to animals than it does to us has not held in his hands an animal fighting for its life. The whole of the being of the animal is thrown into that fight, without reserve. When you say that the fight lacks a dimension of intellectual or imaginative horror, I agree. It is not the mode of being of animals to have an intellectual horror: their whole being is in the living flesh.

"If I do not convince you, that is because my words, here, lack the power to bring home to you the wholeness, the unabstracted, unintellectual nature, of that animal being. That is why I urge you to read the poets who return the living, electric being to language; and if the poets do not move you, I urge you to walk, flank to flank, beside the beast that is prodded down the chute to his executioner.

"You say that death does not matter to an animal because the animal does not understand death. I am reminded of one of the academic philosophers I read in preparing for yesterday's lecture. It was a depressing experience. It awoke in me a quite Swiftian response. If this is the best that human philosophy can offer, I said to myself, I would rather go and live among horses.

"Can we, asked this philosopher, strictly speaking, say that the veal calf misses its mother? Does the veal calf have enough of a

---

[7] *Summa* 2.65.3, quoted in Regan and Singer, *Animal Rights*, 120.

grasp of the significance of the mother-relation, does the veal calf have enough of a grasp of the meaning of maternal absence, does the veal calf, finally, know enough about missing to know that the feeling it has is the feeling of missing?[8]

"A calf who has not mastered the concepts of presence and absence, of self and other—so goes the argument—cannot, strictly speaking, be said to miss anything. In order to, strictly speaking, miss anything, it would first have to take a course in philosophy. What sort of philosophy is this? Throw it out, I say. What good do its piddling distinctions do?

"To me, a philosopher who says that the distinction between human and nonhuman depends on whether you have a white or a black skin, and a philosopher who says that the distinction between human and nonhuman depends on whether or not you know the difference between a subject and a predicate, are more alike than they are unlike.

"Usually I am wary of exclusionary gestures. I know of one prominent philosopher who states that he is simply not prepared to philosophize about animals with people who eat meat. I am not sure I would go as far as that—frankly, I have not the courage—but I must say I would not fall over myself to meet the gentleman whose book I just have been citing. Specifically, I would not fall over myself to break bread with him.

"Would I be prepared to discuss ideas with him? That really is the crucial question. Discussion is possible only when there is common ground. When opponents are at loggerheads, we say: 'Let them reason together, and by reasoning clarify what their differences are, and thus inch closer. They may seem to share nothing else, but at least they share reason.'

"On the present occasion, however, I am not sure I want to concede that I share reason with my opponent. Not when reason

[8] Leahy, *Against Liberation*, 218. Leahy elsewhere argues against a ban on the slaughtering of animals on the grounds that (a) it would bring about unemployment among abattoir workers, (b) it would entail an uncomfortable adjustment to our diet, and (c) the countryside would be less attractive without its customary flocks and herds fattening themselves as they wait to die (214).

is what underpins the whole long philosophical tradition to which he belongs, stretching back to Descartes and beyond Descartes through Aquinas and Augustine to the Stoics and Aristotle. If the last common ground that I have with him is reason, and if reason is what sets me apart from the veal calf, then thank you but no thank you, I'll talk to someone else."

That is the note on which Dean Arendt has to bring the proceedings to a close: acrimony, hostility, bitterness. He, John Bernard, is sure that is not what Arendt or his committee wanted. Well, they should have asked him before they invited his mother. He could have told them.

IT IS past midnight, he and Norma are in bed, he is exhausted, at six he will have to get up to drive his mother to the airport. But Norma is in a fury and will not give up. "It's nothing but food-faddism, and food-faddism is always an exercise in power. I have no patience when she arrives here and begins trying to get people, particularly the children, to change their eating habits. And now these absurd public lectures! She is trying to extend her inhibiting power over the whole community!"

He wants to sleep, but he cannot utterly betray his mother. "She's perfectly sincere," he murmurs.

"It has nothing to do with sincerity. She has no self-insight at all. It is because she has so little insight into her motives that she seems sincere. Mad people are sincere."

With a sigh he enters the fray. "I don't see any difference," he says, "between her revulsion from eating meat and my own revulsion from eating snails or locusts. I have no insight into my motives and I couldn't care less. I just find it disgusting."

Norma snorts. "You don't give public lectures producing pseudophilosophical arguments for not eating snails. You don't try to turn a private fad into a public taboo."

"Perhaps. But why not try to see her as a preacher, a social reformer, rather than as an eccentric trying to foist her preferences on to other people?"

"You are welcome to see her as a preacher. But take a look at all the other preachers and their crazy schemes for dividing mankind up into the saved and the damned. Is that the kind of company you want your mother to keep? Elizabeth Costello and her Second Ark, with her dogs and cats and wolves, none of whom, of course, has ever been guilty of the sin of eating flesh, to say nothing of the malaria virus and the rabies virus and the HI virus, which she will want to save so that she can restock her Brave New World."

"Norma, you're ranting."

"I'm not ranting. I would have more respect for her if she didn't try to undermine me behind my back, with her stories to the children about the poor little veal calves and what the bad men do to them. I'm tired of having them pick at their food and ask, 'Mom, is this veal?' when it's chicken or tuna-fish. It's nothing but a power-game. Her great hero Franz Kafka played the same game with his family. He refused to eat this, he refused to eat that, he would rather starve, he said. Soon everyone was feeling guilty about eating in front of him, and he could sit back feeling virtuous. It's a sick game, and I'm not having the children play it against me."[9]

"A few hours and she'll be gone, then we can return to normal."

"Good. Say goodbye to her from me. I'm not getting up early."

SEVEN o'clock, the sun just rising, and he and his mother are on their way to the airport.

"I'm sorry about Norma," he says. "She has been under a lot of strain. I don't think she is in a position to sympathize. Perhaps one could say the same for me. It's been such a short visit, I

[9] "What [Kafka] required was a regimen of eccentric food habits that were at odds with the 'normal' dinner table habits of his family. . . . Kafka's form of anorexia—not to lose weight but to use food ritualistically as a form of superior statement—was a way of bridging the gap between himself and his family, while at the same time insisting on his uniqueness, his superiority, his sense of rejection." Karl, *Franz Kafka*, 188.

haven't had time to make sense of why you have become so intense about the animal business."

She watches the wipers wagging back and forth. "A better explanation," she says, "is that I have not told you why, or dare not tell you. When I think of the words, they seem so outrageous that they are best spoken into a pillow or into a hole in the ground, like King Midas."

"I don't follow. What is it you can't say?"

"It's that I no longer know where I am. I seem to move around perfectly easily among people, to have perfectly normal relations with them. Is it possible, I ask myself, that all of them are participants in a crime of stupefying proportions? Am I fantasizing it all? I must be mad! Yet every day I see the evidences. The very people I suspect produce the evidence, exhibit it, offer it to me. Corpses. Fragments of corpses that they have bought for money.

"It is as if I were to visit friends, and to make some polite remark about the lamp in their living room, and they were to say, 'Yes, it's nice, isn't it? Polish-Jewish skin it's made of, we find that's best, the skins of young Polish-Jewish virgins.' And then I go to the bathroom and the soap-wrapper says, 'Treblinka—100% human stearate.' Am I dreaming, I say to myself? What kind of house is this?

"Yet I'm not dreaming. I look into your eyes, into Norma's, into the children's, and I see only kindness, human-kindness. Calm down, I tell myself, you are making a mountain out of a molehill. This is life. Everyone else comes to terms with it, why can't you? *Why can't you?*"

She turns on him a tearful face. What does she want, he thinks? Does she want me to answer her question for her?

They are not yet on the expressway. He pulls the car over, switches off the engine, takes his mother in his arms. He inhales the smell of cold cream, of old flesh. "There, there," he whispers in her ear. "There, there. It will soon be over."

REFLECTIONS

Marjorie Garber

> "We are here tonight," he informed the audience, "to listen to a lecture."
>
> Kingsley Amis, *Lucky Jim*

THE TANNER LECTURES sponsored by the Princeton University Center for Human Values were organized this year with special attention to disciplinarity and its discontents. Novelist John Coetzee's two lectures, "The Philosophers and the Animals" and "The Poets and the Animals," met with responses from four scholars with widely different disciplinary (or interdisciplinary) trainings: an animal ethicist, a biologist, a historian of religion, and a literary critic.

Even within Coetzee's lecture-narratives themselves, we might note, some characters express anxiety about disciplines and their authority. The college president, we learn, used to be a political scientist. (What is he *now?*) "That's just anthropology," scoffs Norma, the philosopher of mind, when the subject of dietary laws comes up. And novelist Elizabeth Costello is equally dismissive of certain social science experiments which she regards as mere imbecilities.

In view of these partitions of knowledge, I thought I had better pose some questions having to do with the disciplines I was trained in or might be supposed to know something about—disciplines like literature, psychoanalysis, gender theory, cultural studies, and Shakespeare (which has emerged in recent years as

73

virtually a discipline unto itself). Here were the questions that came to my mind.

- What does the form have to do with the content?

This is a central question for all literary critics, of whatever generation and vintage—and with a novelist of this skill and artfulness (I mean John Coetzee, not Elizabeth Costello) it's a consistently rewarding one.

So, "What does the form of these lectures have to do with the content?" was my first question.

And my second, prompted by psychoanalysis, was:

- What does the form of these lectures displace, repress, or disavow? What is striking in its absence here?
- What are the relationships between the sexes, and between family members, in Coetzee's narrative?

This was a third kind of question, a gender-and-sexuality question. Why should a classic sexual triangle of the *human* social and cultural world (mother-son-son's wife) animate an argument about animals?

And this led me to yet another question, driven by my own recent interest in animal-human relations and what I've called "dog love":[1]

- What does the emphasis on animals tell us about *people*?

You'll see that in a way this is a version of the displacement question. But it is also built into the very form and content of Coetzee's *Lives of Animals*, from the concern about Holocaust analogies to the framing of the whole narrative between references—at the beginning and the end—to the mother's arrival at and departure from the airport and to her "old flesh." If she's flying, she's also dying.

Finally, and most crucially perhaps for this occasion, which was, after all, a series sponsored by the Center for Human *Values*:

[1] Marjorie Garber, *Dog Love* (New York: Simon & Schuster, 1996).

- What, if anything, is the "value" of literary study in today's academy and today's world? Is literary analysis a human value?

In the next few pages I will hazard some very brief answers to each of these sweeping questions.

LET ME BEGIN with the one particular moment in the lectures we heard that struck me especially forcefully with its experiential truth—the moment when the narrator, John Bernard, a young, untenured professor of physics and astronomy, imagines the kind of audience that will attend his mother's *second* talk. "The English department is staging it," he tells his wife. "They are holding it in a seminar room, so I don't think they are expecting a big audience." As a member of an English department myself, I easily recognized this note of skepticism about the size of audiences for literary topics. (On the occasion of the Tanner Lectures at Princeton, in fact, the large lecture hall was full.)

"Writers teach us more than they are aware of," observes Costello. She is ostensibly talking about the poet Ted Hughes. And,"The book we read isn't the book he thought he was writing," she says. She is ostensibly talking about Wolfgang Köhler's *Mentality of Apes*. But she is also—could anything be clearer?— talking about the author of *The Lives of Animals*. Who, like Elizabeth Costello, is a novelist addressing an audience of college students and faculty. Costello herself, like Coetzee, the author of *Foe*, is celebrated for her rewriting of a classic—in her case Joyce's *Ulysses*.

The frame story—the metafiction so familiar and delightful to readers of Coetzee—is deftly established.

> On the basis of her reputation as a novelist [she] has been invited to Appleton to speak on any subject she elects; and she has responded by electing to speak, not about herself and her fiction, as her sponsors would no doubt prefer, but about a hobbyhorse of hers, animals.

It's perfect; even to the term "hobbyhorse," which means both obsession and horse costume, the figurative and the literal bound up together in a way that will reveal itself as characteristic within these deceptively transparent lectures.

The debate with philosophy Professor O'Hearne is set up, we learn, rather like the Tanner Lectures. A text has been circulated in advance: "Since O'Hearne has had the courtesy to send her a précis beforehand, she knows, broadly speaking, what he will be saying." Broadly speaking indeed. Some things have been added and omitted—and such additions and omissions, such traces and overlaps, are the very stuff of literary analysis.

After Elizabeth Costello's first lecture, "The Philosophers and the Animals," her son concludes that the event has been an oddity: "A strange ending to a strange talk, he thinks, ill gauged, ill argued. Not her métier, argumentation. She should not be here." Is this authorial self-abnegation? An escape clause written in advance by a novelist who has consented to speak in an academic venue? A droll resistance to an imagined critique? Or an explanation of the path not taken, a tacit rationale for the novelist's decision to speak in and through a fictional frame?

These lectures and responses, in short—the lectures and responses that were initially presented to the audience in a Princeton University lecture hall—have already been anticipated, fictionalized, and appropriated. A lecture within a lecture; a response within a response. What is the strategy of such an appropriation? Among other things, it is a strategy of *control*.

I CONFESS that I have always been a great fan of metatextual fiction—fiction about fictions, fiction that embodies and builds itself around a hall of mirrors, a *mise en abîme*. So it was with a special flush of pleasure that I recognized these two lectures as belonging to that most accomplished and most maligned of modern literary genres, the academic novel. (Or in this case, perhaps, the academic novella.)

The academic novel is one of the most brilliant minor genres of our time. I say "minor" without intending any disparagement: there is no more pleasurable reading, at least for academics. The acknowledged classics of the genre are Kingsley Amis's *Lucky Jim* and Randall Jarrell's *Pictures from an Institution*, both of them, as it happens, published in 1954, one in England and one in the United States. No one who has read "Lucky" Jim Dixon's account of "Merrie England," delivered (at the behest of his tenured senior colleague) as his first—and perhaps last— public lecture, is likely to forget it. "The point about Merrie England is that it was about the most un-Merrie period in our history."[2]

Some of my other favorites from recent years are David Lodge's *Changing Places* (in which American Morris Zapp of Euphoria College and Briton Philip Swallow of the University of Rummidge exchange jobs and wives); Robert Barnard's murder mystery *The Old Goat*, in which a pompous and ill-tempered English academic visits Australia; and Carolyn Heilbrun's *Death in a Tenured Position*, in which the first tenured woman in the Harvard English department comes to an untimely end. (This particular text has had a special significance for me; on the occasion of my own arrival at Harvard in 1981, where I was—as it happens— the first woman to take up a tenured appointment in the Department of English, I received several copies of Heilbrun's novel in the mail. I would like to believe that they came from well-wishers.)

In any case the tendency of the academic novel to merge with the murder mystery (think of Dorothy Sayers's *Gaudy Night* or Michael Innes's *Death at the President's Lodging* or Rosamond Smith's *Nemesis*) is itself a symptom of culture. The familiar elements of the genre include a beleaguered or bemused junior faculty member, usually from a department of the humanities, a pompous senior colleague, an oblivious college president, several other faculty members including at least one with a German name and another with an exotic European accent, and one or two fresh-faced undergraduates.

---

[2] Kingsley Amis, *Lucky Jim* (1954; London and New York: Penguin Books, 1992), 227.

Perhaps closest to Coetzee's Appleton College (located in the town of Waltham—a conflation, perhaps, of Lawrence University in Appleton, Wisconsin, and Brandeis University in Waltham, Massachusetts) is poet Randall Jarrell's inspired description of the barely fictional Benton College for women (think southern Vermont). In *Pictures from an Institution* a wickedly witty female novelist, spending a year teaching creative writing, takes the occasion to write a tell-all academic novel. "Gertrude felt that the rhythms of academic conversation have been neglected by novelists; that whatever you say against novelists, you have to give them credit for *that*."[3] Thus she resolutely submits to a conversation with the college president, who insists on talking to her about novels ("now she was Collecting for the Book"),[4] and goads the resident painter, who paints feral animals in jungles and marshes, to reveal the identity of his favorite writer, D. H. Lawrence. ("Gertrude smiled and said to him, 'You're older than I thought.'")[5] As in *The Lives of Animals*, a young male junior professor and his wife are what used to be called the "focalizers"—the people through whom we see events unfold.

THE English department of Appleton College holds its seminars in a room in Stubbs Hall, named, we can perhaps imagine (though the text never tells us so) after George Stubbs, the great English painter of horses, dogs, and their keepers. The first draft of John Coetzee's *The Lives of Animals* was full of quiet jokes of this kind, some of which have been amended or edited in the later process of writing. The president's elegant wife, Olivia Garrard, was orginally named Renée Garrard (*not* the same as a certain male comparatist at Stanford); the dean is a man called Arendt (*not* the same as a certain female philosopher). There is a scholar named Elaine Marx (with an *x*, as in Louis Marx Hall, the home of the Princeton University Center for Human Values), who is

[3] Randall Jarrell, *Pictures from an Institution* (1954; Chicago and London: University of Chicago Press, 1986), 41.

[4] Ibid., 44.

[5] Ibid., 233.

not the same as Elaine Marks, the translator of *Modern French Feminisms* but is instead the chair of the English department, a feminist who writes about women's fiction—a description that might fit Princeton English professor (and former department chair) Elaine Showalter. These are "in" jokes for literary scholars—jokes I would call "academic" if the word were not so consistently ironized throughout.

For novelist Elizabeth Costello seems to have little time for "academics." She describes the short and unhappy life of the mathematician Ramanujan, who, "unable to tolerate the climate . . . and the academic regime" in Cambridge (England) died prematurely at the age of thirty-three. She tells the tale of Kafka's domesticated ape Red Peter, who demonstrates a command of "lecture-hall etiquette and academic rhetoric." She deplores the academic totalitarianism with which an "orthodox" interpretation of Swift's *Modest Proposal* is "stuffed down the throat of young readers." She alludes twice, drily and unmistakably, to what she calls "academic philosophers." "Academic" is clearly a suspect term.

The genre of these lectures, then, is metafiction, and together they constitute a version of the academic novel, though crucially this one is suffused with pathos rather than comedy. The effect is to insulate the warring "ideas" (about animal rights, about consciousness, about death, about the family, about academia) against claims of authorship and authority. They are put in play by characters who—precisely because they are "academics"—can be relied upon to be unreliable: both too vehement and too wishy-washy, expert in debaters' points and classroom hyperbole. "Sincerity," assuming it to be a value, cannot be assumed in this contest of faculties. We don't know whose voice to believe.

BUT WHY is the debate about the "lives of animals" so clearly staged as a debate between poetry and philosophy, and why does philosophy seem so clearly to dominate, if not to win? Another familiar genre to which Coetzee's lectures are related is, of course, the philosophical dialogue. It is Plato who most famously invites the comparison of poet and philosopher, and not to the advantage of the poet. On the other hand, poet John Keats once wrote in a letter that poetry "is not so fine a thing as philosophy—For the same reason that an eagle is not so fine a thing as a truth."[6] It's hard to know exactly where Keats's admiration and his irony reside.

Coetzee's first lecture is titled "The Philosophers and the Animals," and the second "The Poets and the Animals." But a good half of the second lecture, and a third of Elizabeth Costello's performance schedule at Appleton College, is given over to discussing philosophy or philosophers, since after her appearance at the English department she takes part in a debate with philosopher Thomas O'Hearne. (Can he be a relative of animal poet and philosopher Vickie Hearne?).

Within the family, too, there is a parallel debate, between the novelist and the philosopher, between Elizabeth and Norma. What are they really fighting about? What is the structural relationship between the mother and the wife—which is to say, between literature and philosophy? Norma's resistance is staged as competition with the mother, and in the closing moments there is an insistence on the word "*normal*"—defined as life without the famous mother on the scene. (Or perhaps life without literature?)

And is the mother—the famous mother—above the battle? I don't think so. John arrives late at his mother's English department seminar, and the minute he comes in she begins to talk about *his* subject, physics, in connection with Rilke's panther poem. Actually, John Bernard and his wife don't really seem very interested in animals—and they don't know a lot about them if they think an older dog is more trouble than a puppy.

A GREAT DEAL of the tension at Appleton College seems to revolve around what Freud called "the seduction of an analogy." This is a matter that goes straight to the heart of the humanities and of

[6] John Keats, letter to George and Georgiana Keats, 14 February–3 May 1819, *Letters of John Keats*, ed. Robert Gittings (New York: Oxford University Press, 1970), 230.

literary and cultural studies. I made a list of figures of speech that appeared in these lectures: donkey's years, scapegoat, close to the bone, stew in their own juice, prick up my ears, easy to digest, baby potatoes. I'm sure I've missed some. Whoever it was who coined the phrase "dead metaphor" could hardly have been more wrong. Is the comparison of human beings to animals venal? Patronizing? A mode of false consciousness? A blasphemy? A necessary mediation? Viewed in literary terms, this is the challenge to humanism.

But there is a larger question: the function of analogy in the posing of some of the most urgent ethical and political questions. At the beginning of "The Poets and the Animals" we are offered the quiet anger of a poet who objects to Elizabeth Costello's analogy between the murdered Jews of Europe and slaughtered cattle. "If Jews were treated like cattle," he says, "it dos not follow that cattle are treated like Jews. The inversion insults the memory of the dead." In protest he absents himself from the dinner in her honor. At the end of "The Poets and the Animals" Elizabeth herself returns, as if compelled, to the horrific image of the Holocaust. She confesses to her son that sometimes she thinks the entire population of the meat-eating world are "participants in a crime of stupefying proportions." And she imagines visiting friends and admiring a lamp in their living room, only to be told that the shade is made of Polish-Jewish female skin.

Whether the Holocaust could ever be part of *any* analogy, much less this one, has been regularly debated and disputed. It is the event beyond analogy, many people say. And yet it is part of oblique and not so oblique analogies every day. Here is an example from recent popular culture.

The children's film *Babe*, about an intelligent and sensitive pig who learns to herd sheep, begins with a scene in a factory shed that directly evokes both German expressionist film and the specter of the Nazi death camps. Low-angled cameras and glaring lights illuminate men dressed in ankle-length lab coats that are evocative of storm-trooper trenchcoats. The men are carrying cattle prods. They descend upon a nursing sow and her piglets and drive her into a truck. The film's voice-over speaks ironically of pig heaven, the place to which all pigs must desire to go, since those that have gone before them seem so content never to return. Suddenly a mechanical milking spigot descends like a bomb in the midst of the remaining piglets. They, too, are marked for slaughter. Babe, the runt, is the only one to survive—and even he narrowly escapes being made into chops and ham in his new life on a family farm. Is this a trivial analogy? Even an insulting one, since pigs, after all, are distinctly non-Kosher? The Holocaust is one profound challenge to the use of analogy.

Coetzee's philosopher O'Hearne alludes briefly to another seductive and painful analogy between animal suffering and human suffering when he dismisses the animal-rights movement as "Western" and falsely universalist. For the animal-protection societies that arose in the nineteenth century were in fact founded by the same social activists who founded the antislavery and woman's suffrage societies. In the United States the Emancipation Proclamation of 1863 was followed by the Thirteenth Amendment in 1865; a year later the American Society for the Prevention of Cruelty to Animals was founded. A similar pattern can be found in Britain, where those who campaigned against slavery were also active in the anticruelty movement. Anna Sewell's *Black Beauty*, published in 1877, was hailed as "the *Uncle Tom's Cabin* of the horse" by the president of the American Humane Society, George Angell. This analogy—to a horse called *black* beauty, after all—was surely capable of giving offense to many American blacks. Again human suffering seems (perhaps) demeaned by comparison with animal suffering. Is this, too, the seduction of an analogy?

But the dangers of figurative language are perhaps most effectively evoked in Coetzee's text through the references to sociobiology, or what Elizabeth Costello refers to as "ethnobiology." In *Not in Our Genes* authors Richard Lewontin, Steven Rose, and Leon J. Kamin argue that one of the errors of sociobiology is to take metaphors for real identities, and to forget (we might say "naturalize") the source of the metaphors. Here they cite in particular two ideas that predate sociobiology but are incorporated into it: the idea of caste in insects and the phenomenon of "slavery" in ants.

These ideas, they say, are transferences from the human realm to the animal or natural realm. (What in linguistics and in literary study is called back-formation, the creation of a new word through the deletion of what is mistakenly understood to be an affix from an existing word: for example, *laze*, a back-formation from *lazy* on the model of *haze* and *hazy*.) "There is a process of backward etymology in sociobiological theory in which human social institutions are laid on animals, metaphorically, and then the human behavior is rederived from the animals as if it were a special case of a general phenomenon that had been independently discovered in other species," they point out. "Does an ant queen (once called a king, before her sex was realized), a totally captive, force-fed, egg-bearing machine, have any resemblance to Elizabeth I or Catherine the Great, or even to the politically powerless but exceedingly rich Elizabeth II?"[7] (*Angels and Insects*, anyone?)

And here is the authors' argument against what they call "false metaphor"—an argument that speaks directly to the use and abuse of literature and literary analysis in culture:

> While sociobiologists inherited royalty and slavery in ants from nineteenth-century entomology, they have made the false metaphor a device of their own. Aggression, warfare, cooperation, kinship, loyalty, coyness, rape, cheating, culture are all applied to nonhuman animals. Human manifestations then come to be seen as special, perhaps more developed, cases.[8]

Let me illustrate this observation with a passage that has always particularly fascinated me from E. O. Wilson's book *Sociobiology* (1975) on the question of what Wilson terms "reciprocal altruism" in nature—a passage that, as you will see, seamlessly

---

[7] R. C. Lewontin, Steven Rose, and Leon J. Kamin, *Not in Our Genes: Biology, Ideology, and Human Nature* (New York: Pantheon Books, 1984), 249.

[8] Ibid., 250.

incorporates tautology, a spectacular example of quotation out of context, and a definition (all too familiar) of poetry as the unproblematic and timeless truth of human nature:

> Selection will discriminate against the individual if cheating has later adverse effects on his life and reproduction that outweigh the momentary advantage gained.

And how does E. O. Wilson support this assertion? He quotes Shakespeare:

> Iago stated the essence in *Othello*: "Good name in man and woman, dear my lord, is the immediate jewel of their souls."[9]

Here Shakespeare quoted out of context equals human nature. Never mind that Iago is lying through his teeth.

"Do YOU really believe, Mother, that poetry classes are going to close down the slaughterhouses?" asks Coetzee's John Bernard, and his mother answers, "No." "Then why do it?" he persists. That is indeed the question.

Poetry makes nothing happen, W. H. Auden once wrote. But is that true? And must it be true? What has poetry to offer, what has language to offer, by way of solace, except analogy, except the art of language? In these two elegant lectures we thought John Coetzee was talking about animals. Could it be, however, that all along he was really asking, "What is the value of literature?"

[9] E. O. Wilson, *Sociobiology: The New Synthesis* (Cambridge: Harvard University Press, 1975), 58.

Peter Singer

❖

WHEN Naomi comes down for breakfast, her father is already at the table. Though there is a bowl of muesli in front of him, his attention is on a typescript that is lying on the table beside him. For Naomi the only unusual aspect of this scene is the depth of her father's frown. She fills her own bowl with muesli, covers it with soymilk, flicks a dangling dreadlock out of it, and breaks the silence:

"Let me guess . . . It's a paper from that graduate student who majored in cultural studies before turning to philosophy?"

"No. This is worse. Not the paper itself—that's really interesting. But it's a more serious problem for me."

"Like?"

"You know how next month I'm going to Princeton to respond to that South African novelist, J. M. Coetzee, who's giving a special lecture about philosophy and animals? This is his lecture. Except that it isn't a lecture at all. It's a fictional account of a female novelist called Costello giving a lecture at an American university."

"You mean that he's going to stand up there and give a lecture about someone giving a lecture? *Très post-moderne*."

"What's postmodern about it?"

"Oh, Dad, where have you been for the past decade? You know, Baudrillard, and all that stuff about simulation, breaking down the distinction between reality and representation, and so on? And look at all the opportunities for playing with self-reference!"

"Call me old-fashioned, then, but I prefer to keep truth and fiction clearly separate. All I want to know is: how am I supposed to reply to this?"

"What does this fictional Costello say about animals, anyway?"

"She's on the right side, no doubt about that. She's a vegetarian. She shows how limited and restrictive some famous scientific inquiries into the minds of apes have been. And there are some very strong passages comparing what we are doing to animals to the Holocaust."

"Oooh, sensitive stuff! I wouldn't equate what the Nazis did to your grandparents with what most people today do to animals."

"Nor would I. But a comparison is not necessarily an equation. Isaac Bashevis Singer has one of his characters compare human behavior toward animals with the Nazis' behavior toward Jews. He's not saying that the crimes are equally evil, but that both are based on the principle that might is right, and the strong can do what they please with those who are in their power."

"That's just a specific example of the parallel between racism and speciesism that you're always making. Is that all Coetzee does with the Holocaust comparison?"

"Costello, you mean. No. She's also saying something about the way in which so many people prefer not to think too much about what is being done to those outside the sphere of the favored group, how we avoid things that might disturb us and look the other way while evil is done. But I think she would go further than that. There's a more radical egalitarianism about humans and animals running through her lecture than I would be prepared to defend."

"A *more* radical egalitarianism?" Naomi raises an eyebrow, tops up her muesli, and continues, "Didn't you write a book the first chapter of which was called 'All Animals are Equal?'"

"I didn't think you'd ever read it."

"Why do I need to read it? I get it from you all the time anyway. Looks like I'm about to get another dose. But I did once get as far as the first page of the first chapter."

"That figures. Anyway, when I say that all animals—all sentient creatures—are equal, I mean that they are entitled to equal consideration of their interests, whatever those interests may be. Pain is pain, no matter what the species of the being that feels it. But I don't say that all animals have the same interests. Species membership may point to things that are morally significant. When it comes to the wrongness of taking life, for example, I've always said that different capacities are relevant to the wrongness of killing."

"That's a relief. When I was little I used to wonder who you would save if the house caught fire, me or Max."

Max had seemed to be asleep on his rug; but at the sound of his name, he lifts his head and looks around expectantly.

Peter kneels by the dog and strokes his neck. "Sorry, Max, but you would have had to fend for yourself. You see, even when she was little, Naomi could wonder about whether I would save her or you. You never wondered about that, did you? And Naomi was always chattering about what she was going to be when she grew up. I'm sure that you don't think about what you will be doing next summer, or even next week."

"And that makes a difference?" It was Naomi, rather than Max, who responded. "What about before I was old enough to think about what I was going to be when I grew up? Would you have tossed a coin—heads I save Naomi, tails I save Max?"

"No, silly. I'm your father, of course I would have saved my lovely baby daughter. But the point is, normal humans have capacities that far exceed those of nonhuman animals, and some of these capacities are morally significant in particular contexts. Look at you. You were up late last night working on your research project, which you have to hand in next month. The topic ceased to excite you long ago, but you are finishing it so that you can get your degree and, if you are lucky, use it to find a job doing something environmentally friendly. Your whole life is future-oriented to a degree that is inconceivable for Max. That gives you much more to lose, and gives an objective reason for anyone—

not just your father—to save you rather than Max if the house catches fire."

"Isn't that still speciesist? Aren't you saying that these characteristics—being self-aware, planning for the future, and so on—are the ones that *humans* have, and therefore they are more valuable than any that *animals* have? Max has a better sense of smell than I do. Why isn't that an objective reason for saving him rather than me?"

"As long as Max is alive, the more happy sniffing he can do, the better. But ask yourself in what way killing—assume that it is painless, unanticipated killing, without any fear beforehand . . ."

Naomi interrupts: "So you're not talking about what really happens in slaughterhouses, then? You've just excluded the overwhelming majority of the deaths that humans inflict on animals. This discussion is becoming purely theoretical."

"Not *purely*. Let me finish. *You* tell *me*: in what way is painless, unanticipated killing wrong in itself?"

"It means the loss of everything. If Max were to be killed, there would be no more doggy-joy of welcoming me home, being taken for a walk, chewing his bone . . ."

"No more of that *for Max*, true. But there are plenty of dog breeders out there who breed dogs to meet the demand. So if we got another puppy from them, thus causing one more dog to come into existence, then there would be just as much of all those good aspects of dog-existence."

"What are you saying—that we could painlessly kill Max, get another puppy to replace him, and everything would be fine? Really, Dad, sometimes you let philosophy carry you away. Too much reasoning, not enough feeling. That's a *horrible* thought."

Naomi is so distressed that Max, who has been listening attentively to the conversation, gets stiffly up from his rug, goes over to her, and starts consolingly licking her bare feet.

"You know very well that I care about Max, so lay off with the 'You reason, so you don't feel' stuff, please. I feel, but I also think about what I feel. When people say we should *only* feel—and at times Costello comes close to that in her lecture—I'm reminded of Göring, who said, 'I think with my blood.' See where it led him. We can't take our feelings as moral data, immune from rational criticism. But to get back to the point, I don't mean that *everything* would be fine if Max were killed and replaced by a puppy. *We* love Max, and *for us* no puppy would replace him. But I asked you why painlessly killing is wrong *in itself.* Our distress is a *side effect* of the killing, not something that makes it wrong in itself. Let's leave Max out of it, since mentioning his name seems to excite him and distress you. Someone once said that pigs have to be thankful that most people are not Jewish, because if all the world were Jewish, there would be no pigs at all . . ."

Naomi interrupts again: "Pigs on factory farms don't need to *thank* anyone for their miserable existence, confined indoors on bare concrete for life. They'd be better off not existing at all."

"You know very well that I'm not defending eating pork, just trying to get a philosophical point across. Let's assume the pigs are leading a happy life and are then painlessly killed. For each happy pig killed, a new one is bred, who will lead an equally happy life. So killing the pig does not reduce the total amount of porcine happiness in the world. What's wrong with it?"

Naomi pauses momentarily. "You're still killing animals with wants of their own. Pigs are as smart as dogs. And I know when Max is looking forward to his walk. Even if he doesn't plan what he'll do next week, he can have short-term wants and anticipations. I bet pigs can too. So we are doing them a wrong by ending their lives, and we don't make up for it when we bring another pig or dog into existence."

Peter smiles triumphantly: "Ah, but now you are conceding my point. We are disagreeing only about the facts of porcine and canine life. And maybe I don't really even disagree with you about that. Suppose I grant that pigs and dogs are self-aware to some degree, and do have thoughts about things in the future. That would provide some reason for thinking it intrinsically wrong to kill them—not absolutely wrong, but perhaps quite a serious wrong. Still, there are other animals—chickens maybe, or fish— who can feel pain but don't have any self-awareness or capacity for thinking about the future. For those animals, you haven't given me any reason why painless killing would be wrong, if other animals take their place and lead an equally good life."

Naomi has finished her breakfast, pushed Max away from her feet, and is lacing up her nonleather Doc Martens. Talking to her father about philosophy always ends up with his switching into lecture mode. Soon she'll be able to get away. But she doesn't want to be rude, so she asks, "And Coetzee doesn't agree with that?"

"Costello doesn't, anyway. She talks about bat-being and human-being both being full of being, and seems to say that their fullness of being is more important than whether it is bat-being or human-being."

"I can see what she's getting at. When you kill a bat, you take away everything that the bat has, its entire existence. Killing a human being can't do more than that."

"Yes, it can. If I pour the rest of this soymilk down the sink, I've emptied the container; and if I do the same to that bottle of Kahlúa you and your friends are fond of drinking when we are out, I'd empty it too. But you'd care more about the loss of the Kahlúa. The value that is lost when something is emptied depends on what was there when it was full, and there is more to human existence than there is to bat existence."

Naomi says quietly: "Oh. I didn't think you'd noticed the Kahlúa." But her father has picked up the paper again and is flipping through the pages. "That's not the worst argument, either. Listen to this. Costello is talking about a book she has written in which she thinks herself into the character of Joyce's Marion Bloom, and then she says,

> If I can think my way into the existence of a being who has never existed, then I can think my way into the existence of a bat or a chimpanzee or an oyster, any being with whom I share the substrate of life."

Naomi is glad to leave the topic of Kahlúa: "You don't have to be a philosopher to see what is wrong with that. The fact that a character doesn't exist isn't something that makes it hard to imagine yourself as that character. You can imagine someone very like yourself, or like someone else you know. Then it is easy to think your way into the existence of that being. But a bat, or an oyster? Who knows? If that's the best argument Coetzee can put up for his radical egalitarianism, you won't have any trouble showing how weak it is."

"But *are* they Coetzee's arguments? That's just the point— that's why I don't know how to go about responding to this so-called lecture. They are *Costello's* arguments. Coetzee's fictional device enables him to distance himself from them. And he has this character, Norma, Costello's daughter-in-law, who makes all the obvious objections to what Costello is saying. It's a marvelous device, really. Costello can blithely criticize the use of reason, or the need to have any clear principles or proscriptions, without Coetzee really committing himself to these claims. Maybe he really shares Norma's very proper doubts about them. Coetzee doesn't even have to worry too much about getting the structure of the lecture right. When he notices that it is starting to ramble, he just has Norma say that Costello is rambling!"

"Pretty tricky. Not an easy thing to reply to. But why don't you try the same trick in response?"

"*Me?* When have I ever written fiction?"

Wendy Doniger

❖

IT SEEMS somehow reductionistic to respond to these deeply moving readings as if they had been dry academic arguments. But all I can do is offer some texts from the other traditions that I know, in support of what I take to be the ideas implicit in J. M. Coetzee's Tanner Lectures—namely, an argument for the inevitable, if unfalsifiable, links between communion with animals, compassion for animals, and the refusal to torment, if not necessarily the refusal to kill and/or eat, animals. Let me begin, as he does, with the eating.

COMPASSION TOWARD ANIMALS, AND VEGETARIANISM

Thomas O'Hearne, one of Elizabeth Costello's critics in the second Tanner Lecture, argues that to treat animals compassionately is "very recent, very Western, and even very Anglo-Saxon," and that we delude ourselves when we think that we can impose this idea on other traditions who are "blind" to it. Elizabeth challenges him too weakly (people keep pets, and children love animals, all over the world). I would make a stronger case for the non-Western religions, though not so strong as most animal-lovers generally assume.

After about the sixth century B.C.E., most Hindus, Buddhists, and Jains did indeed feel that people should not eat animals, in part, as is generally argued, because they themselves might be reborn as animals, but more because they feared that animals might retaliate in the afterworld. A Vedic text from 900 B.C.E. tells of a boy who went to "the world beyond" (that is, the world to which one goes after death—the theory of rebirth is not yet reflected in this text) and saw a man cut another man to pieces and eat him, and another man "eating a man who was screaming," and another man "eating a man who was *soundlessly* screaming." When he returned to earth, his father explained that the first man represented people who, when they had been in *this* world, had cut down trees and burnt them, the second people who had cooked for themselves animals that cry out, and the third people who had cooked for themselves rice and barley, which scream soundlessly.[1]

Now, we might regard this as an extreme ecological program—to ban not only the eating of animals, but the burning of fuel and the consumption of vegetables (there was one Hindu, in the twentieth century, who claimed to have recorded the screams of carrots that were strapped down to a table and chopped up). But in fact this is not what this text argues for. When the terrified boy asked his father, "How can one avoid that fate?" his father told him that he could easily avoid it simply by offering oblations to the gods before consuming fuel, animals, and vegetables. This is an example of the rationalization attributed to the Greeks in Elizabeth's argument with Wunderlich in the first lecture: invent the gods and blame *them*.

Other parts of this same text do express a kind of submerged guilt at the slaughter of animals, perhaps even compassion, though the ostensible point of the myth is to justify the slaughter: in the beginning, cattle had the skin that humans have now, and humans had the skin that cattle have now. Cattle could not bear the heat, rain, flies, and mosquitoes, and asked humans to change skins with them; in return, they said, "You can eat us and use our skin for your clothing." And so it was. And the sacrificer puts on the red hide of a cow so that, when he goes to the other world, cattle do not eat him; otherwise, they would eat

---

[1] *Jaiminiya Brahmana* 1.42–44; Wendy Doniger O'Flaherty, *Tales of Sex and Violence: Folklore, Sacrifice, and Danger in the Jaiminiya Brahmana* (Chicago: University of Chicago Press, 1985), 32–35.

him.[2] Another common ploy to assuage guilt—which is to say, to silence compassion—was to assert that the animal willingly sacrificed itself.[3] On yet other occasions an attempt was made to convince the animal that it was not in fact killed. Thus in the hymn of the horse sacrifice in the *Rig Veda*, ca. 1000 B.C.E., the priest says to the horse, "You do not really die through this, nor are you harmed. You go on paths pleasant to go on."[4]

Hindu legal texts generated a great deal of what we now call "language" to sidestep this deep ambivalence. The most famous of these texts, *The Laws of Manu*, composed in the early centuries of the Common Era, ricochets back and forth between the vegetarian and sacrificial stances:

> As many hairs as there are on the body of the sacrificial animal that he kills for no (religious) purpose here on earth, so many times will he, after his death, suffer a violent death in birth after birth. The Self-existent one himself created sacrificial animals for sacrifice; sacrifice is for the good of this whole (universe); and therefore killing in a sacrifice is not killing. Herbs, sacrificial animals, trees, animals (other than sacrificial animals), and birds who have been killed for sacrifice win higher births again. On the occasion of offering the honey-mixture (to a guest), at a sacrifice, and in rituals in which the ancestors are the deities, and only in these circumstances, should sacrificial animals suffer violence, but not on any other occasion; this is what Manu has said.[5]

---

[2] See the story of "How Men Changed Skins with Animals," *Jaiminiya Brahmana* 2.182–83; also in O'Flaherty, *Tales of Sex and Violence*. For a discussion of this genre of prevarication in other religions, see Jonathan Z. Smith, "The Bare Facts of Ritual," in *Imagining Religion* (Chicago: University of Chicaog Press, 1982), 53–65.

[3] See the discussion of the willingness of the sacrificed animal in Wendy Doniger O'Flaherty, "The Good and Evil Shepherd," in *Gilgul: Essays on Transformation, Revolution, and Permanence in the History of Religions, Dedicated to Zwi Werblowsky*, ed. S. Shaked, D. Shulman, and G. G. Stromsa (Leiden: E. J. Brill, 1987), 169–91.

[4] *Rig Veda* 1.162.21; Wendy Doniger O'Flaherty, *The Rig Veda: An Anthology, 108 Hymns Translated from the Sanskrit* (Harmondsworth: Penguin Classics, 1981), 91.

[5] *The Laws of Manu* 5.38–41; *The Laws of Manu*, a new translation of the *Manavadharmasastra*, by Wendy Doniger, with Brian K. Smith (Harmondsworth: Penguin Classics, 1991), 103.

Outside the sacrificial arena, the cow that generously gives her milk replaces the steer that must be slaughtered to provide food;[6] Hindu myths imagine the transition from hunting to farming, from killing to milking, from blood sacrifice to vegetable sacrifice.[7]

We may see a variant of this argument in a part of *Gulliver's Travels* that Elizabeth does not cite in her evocation of this text. When Gulliver finds himself unable to live on either the vegetarian fare of the Houyhnhnms or the flesh that is the food of the horrid Yahoos, he devises a solution: "I observed a cow passing by; whereupon I pointed to her, and expressed a desire to let me go and milk her." Henceforth Gulliver survives, in perfect health, on a diet of milk and a bread made of oats—two civilized alternatives to the two natural extremes of raw flesh and grass.

In Hindu myths of this genre, the humans among the animals eat "fruits and roots"; in the Buddhist variants, they eat nothing at all (not being true humans yet) or they eat the earth itself, which is delicious and nourishing, and is sometimes called the earth-cow. [8] (Shame, too, a factor that Elizabeth's son John interjects into the argument, enters in here: when people begin to hoard the food given by the earth-cow, they build houses to hide both the food and their newly discovered sexuality; for people who watch others copulating say, "How could anyone treat someone else like that?" and throw clods of earth at them.)[9] These two strategies, one realistic and one fantastic, provide natural alternatives to the food that men do in fact share with *unmythical* animals: meat.

But it is not quite so simple. Vegetarianism and compassion for animals are not the same thing at all. Elizabeth Costello vividly

[6] Wendy Doniger O'Flaherty, *Women, Androgynes, and Other Mythical Beasts* (Chicago: University of Chicago Press, 1980), 239–54.

[7] Wendy Doniger O'Flaherty, *Other Peoples' Myths: The Cave of Echoes* (New York: Macmillan, 1988; reprint, University of Chicago Press, 1995), 82–96.

[8] Wendy Doniger O'Flaherty, *The Origins of Evil in Hindu Mythology* (Berkeley and Los Angeles: University of California Press, 1976), 29, 321–46.

[9] *Digha Nikaya*, Aggañña Suttanta 27.10; *Visuddhimagga* 13.49; cited by O'Flaherty, *Origins of Evil*, 33.

reminds us that it is usual for most *individuals* to eat meat without killing animals (most nonvegetarians, few of whom hunt or butcher, do it every day) and equally normal for an individual to kill without eating the kill—or, indeed, any other meat (what percentage of hit men or soldiers devour their fallen enemies?). Indeed, one historian of ancient India has suggested that vegetarianism and killing were originally mutually exclusive: that in the earliest period of Indian civilization, meat-eating householders would, in time of war, consecrate themselves as warriors by giving up the eating of meat.[10] They either ate meat *or* killed. In later Hinduism, the strictures against eating and killing continued to work at odds, so that it was regarded as better (for most people, in general: the rules would vary according to the caste status of the person in each case) to kill an Untouchable than to kill a Brahmin, but better to eat a Brahmin (presuming that one came across a dead one) than to eat an Untouchable (under the same circumstances). It is within this world of revisionist scripture and unresolved ambivalence that we must come to terms with Gandhi's twisted vegetarianism—rightly problematized by "the blond man" who argues with Norma.

Nevertheless, the logical assumption that any animal that one ate had to have been killed by *someone* led to a natural association between the ideal of vegetarianism and the ideal of nonviolence toward living creatures. And this ideal came to prevail in India, reinforced by the idea of reincarnation and its implication that humans and animals were part of a single system of the recycling of souls: do not kill an animal, for it might be your grandmother, or your grandchild, or you.

COMPASSION TOWARD ANIMALS, AND INDIVIDUAL HUMAN SALVATION

But compassion for animals is seldom the dominant factor in South Asian arguments for vegetarianism. Buddhists and Jains

---

[10] Jan Heesterman, *The Inner Conflict of Tradition* (Chicago: University of Chicago Press, 1985).

cared, like Elizabeth Costello, for individual human salvation, more, really, than they cared for animals; they refrained from killing and eating animals to protect their own souls from pollution (and even, as Norma nastily but correctly points out, to protect their bodies from social pollution). Yet it seems to me that this argument for individual salvation could be adopted in a secular form in the Western conversation more often than it is. It is an argument often made against capital punishment, that it should be abolished not because of its evil effects upon criminals but because it is bad for *us*, bad for us to be a people who kill people like that. So, too, whether or not we can argue that killing animals for food or experimentation is bad for the universe, for the food supply, for medical advances, or even whether or not we can prove that animals suffer as we do, or know that they are going to die, we might take from the South Asian context the very wise argument that *we* know that they are going to die, and that *that* makes it bad for us to kill them.

COMPASSION FOR ANIMALS AS NONOTHER

Let me turn now to the argument, implicit in the rebirth scenario, that we must not kill and eat animals because they are like us. In India, this argument begins the other way around: the Vedic myths of sacrifice (before the theory of rebirth) close the gap between humans and animals in the other direction, by including humans with animals as sacrificial beasts. The Sanskrit term *Pashu* (cognate with Latin *pecus*, cattle [as in Pecos Bill or impecunious—meaning having no cattle, no bread, no money]) designates sacrificial and domestic animals, animals that we keep until we slaughter them, either in ritual or for food, or both. These are the animals that we own and measure ourselves by; they are the animals that are us. *Mriga*, related to the verb "to hunt" (*margayati*, from which is also derived the noun *marga*, "a trail or path"), designates any animal that we hunt, in particular a deer. But just as "deer" in English comes from the German *Tier*, meaning any wild animal, a meaning that persisted in English for some time

(Shakespeare used the phrase "small deer" in this sense), so too in Sanskrit the paradigmatic *mriga*, the wild animal par excellence, is the deer, just as the paradigmatic *pashu* is the cow (or, more precisely, the bull). But *mriga* is also the general term for any wild animal in contrast with any tame beast or *pashu*. *Pashu*s are the animals that get sacrificed, whatever their origins; *mriga*s are the animals that get hunted. In both cases, the ancient Indians defined animals according to the manner in which they killed them.

The Vedas and Brahmanas often list five basic kinds of sacrificial animal or *pashu*: bull (*go*, which can also mean "cow"), horse, billygoat, ram, and human being (person, particularly male person or man).[11] The later Vedic tradition then opens the gap by distinguishing humans from animals in sacrificing only animals; *The Laws of Manu* lists *pashu*s, *mriga*s, and humans as three separate groups—though one Hindu commentator glosses this by saying that, even though humans are in fact *pashu*s, they are mentioned separately because of their special preeminence.[12] And still later Hinduism once again narrows the gap between humans and animals by joining humans and animals together as creatures *not* to be sacrificed, in contrast with vegetables (which remain stubbornly other).[13]

To imply that humans are sacrificial victims just like other animals, and to imply that neither humans nor animals should be sacrificial victims, are two very different ways of expressing the belief that we are like animals. So, too, the decision not to kill and/or eat animals follows from the belief that, since animals are nonother, to eat them is a kind of cannibalism. On the other hand, the belief that animals are *so* other as to be gods gives yet another swing to the pendulum and produces a reason to eat such animals after all—to eat them ritually, which lands us back at square one. The argument that humans (but not animals) are

---

[11] *Atharva Veda* 11.2.9, with Sayana's commentary.

[12] Govindaraja on *Manu* 1.39. In *Manu-Smrti, with Nine Commentaries*, ed. Jayantakrishna Harikrishna Dave (Bombay: Bharatiya Vidya Series, no. 29, 1975).

[13] O'Flaherty, *Other Peoples' Myths*, 82–83.

created in the image of god is often used in the West to justify cruelty to animals, but most mythologies assume that animals, *rather than humans*, are the image of god—which may be a reason *to eat them*.

The belief that animals are like us in some essential way is the source of the enduring and widespread myth of a magic time or place or person that erases the boundary between humans and animals. The place is like the Looking-Glass forest where things have no names, where Alice could walk with her arms around the neck of a fawn. The list of people who live at peace among animals would include Enkidu in the epic of *Gilgamesh* and the many mythical children who are raised as cubs by a pack of animals, like Romulus and Remus, Mowgli, and Tarzan, like Pecos Bill (suckled by a puma) and Davy Crockett (raised among mountain lions). T. H. White, translator of a medieval bestiary, imagined the young King Arthur's education by Merlin the magician as taking place among ants and geese and owls and badgers.[14] This myth is very different from the mythologies of bestiality, which imagine a very different sort of intimacy (though the two intersect uncomfortably in the image of "lying down with" animals, literally sleeping with animals).[15] Our myths generally do *not* define animals as those with whom we do not have sex (though the president's elegant wife, Olivia Garrard, favors this distinction).

The ideal state of humans among animals is not one in which wild animals become tame (like Elsa the Lioness in *Born Free*, or the Lone Ranger's horse Silver). It is a state in which a human becomes one of the animals. Or rather, more precisely, a human becomes part of the society of the animals but remains a human, like Barbara Smuts among the nonhuman primates; the adopted child in the myth must eventually return to the human world. In

[14] T. H. White, *The Once and Future King* (London: Fontana Books, 1962); pt. 1, "The Sword in the Stone." The culmination of the animal education comes in chap. 23.

[15] Wendy Doniger O'Flaherty, "The Mythology of Masquerading Animals, or, Bestiality" (in *In the Company of Animals*, ed. Arien Mack, *Social Research: An International Quarterly of the Social Sciences* 62, no. 3 [Fall 1995]: 751–72).

contrast with the rituals of cultural transformation, in which we cease to eat flesh by becoming quintessentially cultural and eating bread or milk instead, these are myths of natural transformation, in which we become quintessentially natural and eat what animals eat (food that may in fact include other animals).

COMPASSION FOR ANIMALS AS CONSCIOUS

Hinduism assumes that animals have transmigrating souls and a consciousness like our own, and that, though they do not have human language, they can communicate with us in other ways that reveal the presence of a mind and a soul. This does not, of course, mean that they think and/or feel precisely as we do; merely that they, too, think and feel. Descartes's assumption that thinking is what makes us what we are is all wrong, as Elizabeth demonstrates.[16]

Elizabeth gives a fine answer to the philosopher Thomas Nagel's provocative question, "What is it like to be a bat?" Long before Nagel, an equine metaphor was used to express the problems that we have in imagining minds of animals. Xenophanes, an ancient Greek philosopher, said, "If cattle and horses or lions had hands, or could draw with their feet, horses would draw the forms of god like horses."[17] The anthropologist Radcliffe-Brown, in conversation with his colleague Max Gluckman, had nicknamed Sir James George Frazer's mode of reasoning (in *The Golden Bough*) the "if I were a horse" argument, from the story of the farmer in the Middle West whose horse had strayed from its paddock. The farmer went into the paddock, chewed some grass, and ruminated, "Now if *I* were a horse, which way would I go?"[18]

---

[16] The reductio ad absurdum of the Cartesian assumption is expressed by the joke about Descartes ordering a cup of coffee, to go, in a Dunkin' Donut shop; when the waitress asked him, "Do you want cream and sugar in that, Mr. Descartes?" he replied, "I think not," and vanished.

[17] Xenophanes, frag. 15, in *Die Fragmente*, ed. Ernst Heitsch (Munich: Artemis Verlag, 1983).

[18] Cited by R. Angus Downie, *Frazer and the Golden Bough* (London: Gollancz, 1970), 42.

The British anthropologist E. E. Evans-Pritchard, in criticizing the introspectionist psychologies of Spencer and Tylor, warned that it was futile to try to imagine how it would feel "if I were a horse."[19] Whatever its merits as a caveat for anthropologists, I would regard the "if I were a horse" fantasy as quite a useful way of dealing with *horses* (like Elizabeth Costello, I am literal-minded). For it is the pious belief of many horsemen (and horsewomen) that they can think like horses.[20] And maybe they can. If the farmer, after chewing grass, lopes off to a field where the grass is much better than the field where he had been keeping his horse, and finds his horse there, perhaps he *has* thought like a horse. On the other hand, he does not have to eat the grass himself when he gets there; he does not have to *feel* like a horse. It is useful to distinguish between ontological relativism and moral relativism; one need not adopt the morals, or the diet, of a horse to understand a horse. Perhaps Nagel changed the horse to a bat to make the point of noncommunication more dramatic, because we don't *love* bats; but that is precisely my point: we can understand horses because we love them (and, tautologically, we love them because we understand them).

Though we can never *know*, for certain, if we or anyone else has really understood how horses think, many people have tried and have persuaded us that they have succeeded. Anna Sewell's *Black Beauty* (sometimes dubbed "the *Uncle Tom's Cabin* of the horse") (1877), Rudyard Kipling's "The Maltese Cat" (1898—the Cat is actually a polo pony) and Leo Tolstoi's "Strider [Xolstomer]" (1894) are narrated by horses (the latter so vividly that it led Maxim Gorky to exclaim to Tolstoi, "You must have been a horse in a previous incarnation"). This line of argument may or may not be good anthropology, but it is good ecology. It argues for the

[19] E. E. Evans-Pritchard, *Theories of Primitive Religion* (Oxford: Clarendon Press, 1965), 24, 43.

[20] See, for example, R. H. Smythe, *The Mind of the Horse* (London: Country Life, 1965); Moyra Williams, *Horse Psychology* (London: Methuen, 1956); and, most recently, Vicki Hearne, *Adam's Task: Calling Animals by Name* (New York: Knopf, 1986).

empathic leap of faith, the Kantian belief that what hurts me hurts you—and hurts horses. The poetry, if not the comparative neurology, persuades me that Coetzee has in fact entered the head of Sultan to discover the better questions that the captive ape might have thought about ("What is wrong with him, what misconception does he have of me, that makes him believe it is easier for me to reach a banana hanging from a wire than to pick up a banana from the floor?" "WHERE IS HOME? HOW DO I GET HOME?"), questions that are so much better (if so much less falsifiable) than "How can I get this banana?"

I have followed Coetzee in shifting the ground from the thoughts of animals to their feelings. There is a justly famous Taoist parable to this effect:

> Chuang Tzu and Hui Tzu had strolled on to the bridge over the Hao, when the former observed, "See how the minnows are darting about! That is the pleasure of fishes." "You not being a fish yourself," said Hui Tzu, "how can you possibly know in what consists the pleasure of fishes?" "And you not being I," retorted Chuang Tzu, "how can you know that I do not know?" "If I, not being you, cannot know what you know," urged Hui Tzu, "it follows that you, not being a fish, cannot know in what consists the pleasure of fishes." "Let us go back," said Chuang Tzu, "to your original question. You asked me how I knew in what consists the pleasure of fishes. Your very question shows that you knew I knew. I knew it from my own feelings on the bridge."[21]

No one can prove that someone else does *not* know how animals feel.

One could, though Coetzee and Elizabeth do not, also argue that animals themselves understand the feelings of other animals, that they themselves have compassion. Dogs and horses certainly do, as anyone knows who has seen their deeply troubled reaction to the sight of a wounded animal of their own or a closely related

---

[21] Chuang Chou, *Chuang-tzu*, bk. 17, par. 13, "Chuang-tzu and Hui-tzu dispute on their understanding of the enjoyment of fishes." *Chuang Tzu: Mystic, Moralist, and Social Reformer*, trans. Herbert A. Giles (London: B. Quaritch, 1926), 218–19.

species. Our empathy cannot be limited by our physical, any more than by our mental, capacities.[22] Elizabeth could feel what a corpse felt; amputees experience pain in the absent limb, the phantom limb. Surely we, too, can experience pain in our paws, in our tails, in our fetlocks and pasterns, perhaps even, if we are truly talented, in our fins and scales.

COMPASSION FOR ANIMALS AS HAVING LANGUAGE

Wittgenstein would, I think, have been skeptical of the "if I were a horse" approach; he argued that "if a lion could talk, we could not understand him."[23] And language is, I think, the place from which compassion springs. We cannot torment (or eat) the people we speak with. Elaine Scarry made this point, in reverse, when she argued that torture takes away speech,[24] and Lewis Carroll made it when the Red Queen, having introduced Alice to the roast ("Alice—mutton: Mutton—Alice"), commanded: "It isn't etiquette to cut any one you've been introduced to. Remove the joint!"[25] And this language need not be even the signing of chimps, let alone the whistles of dolphins (or the body language of primates that Barbara Smuts learns to read); it may be no more than the silent language of the eyes. Emmanuel Levinas once said that the face of the other says, Don't kill me.[26] This is the language that we must learn to read, and the language that is denied by people who defend the right to treat animals as things, through a self-serving tautology. Elizabeth Costello speaks of animals that

[22] I once fainted dead away at a circumcision; apparently my foreskin recoiled in horror of the cut; contrariwise, many men have fainted away during their wives' childbirth pains, and not merely in societies that ritually enshrine the couvade.

[23] Ludwig Wittgenstein, *Philosophical Investigations*, 3d ed., trans. G.E.M. Anscombe (New York: Prentice Hall, 1958), 223.

[24] Elaine Scarry, *The Body in Pain: The Making and Unmaking of the World* (New York: Oxford University Press, 1985).

[25] Lewis Carroll, *Through the Looking-Glass*, chap. 9, "Queen Alice."

[26] Emmanuel Levinas, *Totality and Infinity: An Essay in Exteriority*, trans. Alphonso Lingis (The Hague: Martinus Nijhoff, 1979), 198–99.

refuse to speak, that keep the dignity of the silence. I disagree: they speak, and we refuse to grant them the dignity of *listening* to them.

Since dolphins are not fish but look like fish, and since they are animals but they talk to us in a way that most other animals cannot, they doubly straddle the boundary between our own categories of mammals and fish and thereby threaten our definition of what it is to be human. This accounts, in part, for some people's reluctance to call what dolphins do "speech." And in fact the language that people use to talk to dolphins is neither the language in which dolphins talk to one another nor the language in which we talk to one another—it is a Rosetta stone language, a kind of mammalian Esperanto. Yet it is a language, and it joins us with the fish.

Often, the myth of the human among wild animals does not tell us what the people and animals eat, but it always tells us how they manage to speak to one another, and how they manage not to attack one another (two closely related problems). Gulliver *asks* the cow, in sign language, for her milk. It is language, not food, that ultimately separates us from the animals, even in myths. Only by speaking their language will we really be able to know how we would think and feel if we were fish or horses.

EPILOGUE

"If Red Peter had any sense, he would not have any children," says Elizabeth. Do animals think like this? Do they want to be sterile? I once met an animal-rights activist, dined with him, and after a while cheerfully began to make friends with him by telling him about my dogs and my horse, and then asking him what pets he had. He said he didn't have pets, thought it was cruel to keep them in a city. I began to apologize for myself ("I take them out to the park to run free with other dogs for hours every day, feed them minced steak, etc., etc.") but had to acknowledge the violence done to them by their restricted freedom, periods of absence from me, and so forth. What would you do? I asked. His answer was simple: neuter all the extant dogs and cats, and in twenty years there would be no more dogs and cats in the world. As with Greek tragic heroes, the ultimate right of all animals—in his view—was never to be born. It seems to me that we can do better than that.

Barbara Smuts

❖

I<small>N THE</small> third Tanner Lecture, Coetzee's protagonist, novelist
Elizabeth Costello, debates the issue of animal rights with philosophy professor Thomas O'Hearne. According to O'Hearne,
"Thomas Aquinas says that friendship between human beings
and animals is impossible, and I tend to agree. You can be friends
neither with a Martian nor with a bat, for the simple reason that
you have too little in common with them." Although Costello
challenges many of O'Hearne's other statements, on this one, so
easily refuted, she remains mysteriously silent. Yet the failure of
Costello—and of Coetzee's other characters—to address Aquinas's claim is not so surprising when we realize that in a story that
is, ostensibly,[1] about our relations with members of other species,
none of the characters ever mentions a personal encounter with
an animal. The closest we come to the possibility of such encounters is when Costello's son says to himself, "If she wants to open
her heart to animals, why can't she stay home and open it to her
cats?" Thus we discover only secondhand that Elizabeth Costello
lives with animals. At no point in her passionate comments on
animal rights does she mention the beings who, in all probability
(given that she is an old woman who lives alone, far from her son)

I thank Peter M. Sherman and Steve Lansing for valuable feedback.

[1] I say "ostensibly" because Coetzee's lectures can be interpreted in many ways, as
indicated most clearly by Garber's commentary (this volume). However, to para-
phrase Elizabeth Costello (in her reflections on the essay "What Is It Like to Be a
Bat?" by philosopher Thomas Nagel), when Coetzee writes about animal rights, I
take him to be writing, in the first place, about animals and our relations with them.

are the individuals with whom she interacts most often and, perhaps, most intimately.

Why doesn't Elizabeth Costello mention her relations with her cats as an important source of her knowledge about, and attitudes toward, other animals? Maybe she feels constrained by the still-strong academic taboo against references to personal experience, although this seems unlikely, given her expressed disdain for so many of the other taboos of rationalism. Whatever her (or Coetzee's) reasons, the lack of reference to real-life relations with animals is a striking gap in the discourse on animal rights contained in Coetzee's text. Entering territory where, perhaps, Costello (and maybe even Coetzee) feared to tread, I will attempt to close this gap, not through formal scientific discourse, but rather, as Elizabeth Costello urges, by speaking from the heart. The heart, says Costello, is "the seat of a faculty, *sympathy*, that allows us to share . . . the being of another." For the heart to truly share another's being, it must be an embodied heart, prepared to encounter directly the embodied heart of another. I have met the "other" in this way, not once or a few times, but over and over during years spent in the company of "persons" like you and me,[2] who happen to be nonhuman.

These nonhuman persons include gorillas at home in the perpetually wet, foggy mountaintops of central Africa, chimpanzees carousing in the hot, rugged hills of Western Tanzania, baboons lazily strolling across the golden grass plains of highland Kenya, and dolphins gliding languorously through the green, clear waters of Shark Bay.[3] In each case, I was lucky to be accepted by

---

[2] The term *person* is commonly used in two different ways: first, as a synonym for human, and, second, to refer to a type of interaction or relationship of some degree of intimacy involving actors who are individually known to one another, as in "personal relationship," knowing someone "personally," or engaging with another "person to person." Here I use the word in the second sense, to refer to any animal, human or nonhuman, who has the capacity to participate in personal relationships, with one another, with humans, or both. I return to the concept of animal "personhood" later in the essay.

[3] Shark Bay is off the coast of Western Australia, the site of a research project on wild bottlenose dolphins.

the animals as a mildly interesting, harmless companion, permitted to travel amongst them, eligible to be touched by hands and fins, although I refrained, most of the time, from touching in turn.

I mingled with these animals under the guise of scientific research, and, indeed, most of my activities while "in the field" were designed to gain objective, replicable information about the animals' lives. Doing good science, it turned out, consisted mostly of spending every possible moment with the animals, watching them with the utmost concentration, and documenting myriad aspects of their behavior. In this way, I learned much that I could confidently report as scientific findings. But while one component of my being was engaged in rational inquiry, another part of me, by necessity, was absorbed in the physical challenge of functioning in an unfamiliar landscape devoid of other humans or any human-created objects save what I carried on my back.[4] When I first began working with baboons, my main problem was learning to keep up with them while remaining alert to poisonous snakes, irascible buffalo, aggressive bees, and leg-breaking pig-holes. Fortunately, these challenges eased over time, mainly because I was traveling in the company of expert guides—baboons who could spot a predator a mile away and seemed to possess a sixth sense for the proximity of snakes. Abandoning myself to their far superior knowledge, I moved as a humble disciple, learning from masters about being an African anthropoid.

Thus I became (or, rather, regained my ancestral right to be) an animal, moving instinctively through a world that felt (because it was) like my ancient home. Having begun to master this challenge, I faced another one equally daunting: to comprehend and behave according to a system of baboon etiquette bizarre and subtle enough to stop Emily Post in her tracks. This task was forced on me by the fact that the baboons stubbornly resisted my feeble but sincere attempts to convince them that I was nothing more than a detached observer, a neutral object they could

---

[4] I spent more time studying baboons than any other species, and so in what follows, I concentrate on my experiences with them.

ignore. Right from the start, they knew better, insisting that I was, like them, a social subject vulnerable to the demands and rewards of relationship. Since I was in their world, they determined the rules of the game, and I was thus compelled to explore the unknown terrain of human-baboon intersubjectivity. Through trial and embarrassing error, I gradually mastered at least the rudiments of baboon propriety. I learned much through observation, but the deepest lessons came when I found myself sharing the being of a baboon[5] because other baboons were treating me like one. Thus I learned from personal experience that if I turned my face away but held my ground, a charging male with canines bared in threat would stop short of attack. I became familiar with the invisible line defining the personal space of each troop member, and then I discovered that the space expands and contracts depending on the circumstances. I developed the knack of sweetly but firmly turning my back on the playful advances of juveniles, conveying, as did the older females, that although I found them appealing, I had more important things to do. After many months of immersion in their society I stopped thinking so much about what to do and instead simply surrendered to instinct, not as mindless, reflexive action, but rather as action rooted in an ancient primate legacy of embodied knowledge.

Living in this way with baboons, I discovered what Elizabeth Costello means when she says that to be an animal is to "be full of being," full of "joy." Like the rest of us, baboons get grouchy, go hungry, feel fear and pain and loss. But during my times with them, the default state seemed to be a lighthearted appreciation of being a baboon body in baboon-land. Adolescent females concluded formal, grown-up-style greetings with somber adult males with a somersault flourish. Distinguished old ladies, unable to get a male's attention, stood on their heads and gazed up at the guy upside down. Grizzled males approached balls of wrestling infants and tickled them. Juveniles spent hours perfecting the technique of swinging from a vine to land precisely on the top of

[5] I refer again to Elizabeth Costello's comments on sharing "the being of another."

mom's head. And the voiceless, breathy chuckles of baboon play echoed through the forest from dawn to dusk.

During the cool, early morning hours, the baboons would work hard to fill their stomachs, but as the temperature rose, they became prone to taking long breaks in especially attractive locales. In a mossy glade or along the white-sanded beach of an inland lake, they would shamelessly indulge a passion for lying around in the shade on their backs with their feet in the air. Every now and then someone would emit a deep sigh of satisfaction. Off and on, they would concur about the agreeableness of the present situation by participating in a chorus of soft grunts that rippled through the troop like a gentle wave. In the early days of my fieldwork when I was still preoccupied with doing things right, I regarded these siestas as valuable opportunities to gather data on who rested near whom. But later, I began to lie around with them. Later still, I would sometimes lie around without them—that is, among them, but while they were still busy eating. Once I fell asleep surrounded by 100 munching baboons only to awaken half an hour later, alone, except for an adolescent male who had chosen to nap by my side (presumably inferring from my deep sleep that I'd found a particularly good resting spot). We blinked at one another in the light of the noonday sun and then casually sauntered several miles back to the rest of the troop, with him leading the way.

There were 140 baboons in the troop, and I came to know every one as a highly distinctive individual. Each one had a particular gait, which allowed me to know who was who, even from great distances when I couldn't see anyone's face. Every baboon had a characteristic voice and unique things to say with it; each had a face like no other, favorite foods, favorite friends, favorite bad habits. Dido, when chased by an unwelcome suitor, would dash behind some cover and then dive into a pig-hole, carefully peeking out every few moments to see if the male had given up the chase. Lysistrata liked to sneak up on an infant riding on its mother's back, knock it off (gently), and then pretend to be deeply preoccupied with eating some grass when mom turned to see the cause of her infant's distress. Apié, the alpha male, would carefully study the local fishermen from a great distance, wait for just the right moment to rush toward them, take a flying leap over their heads to land on the fish-drying rack, grab the largest fish, and disappear into the forest before anyone knew what was happening.

I also learned about baboon individuality directly, since each one approached his or her relationship with me in a slightly different way. Cicero, the outcast juvenile, often followed me and sat quietly a few feet away, seemingly deriving some small comfort from my proximity. Leda, the easygoing female, would walk so close to me I could feel her fur against my bare legs. Dakar, feisty adolescent male, would catch my eye and then march over to me, stand directly in front of me, and grab my kneecap while staring at my face intently (thanks to Dakar, I've become rather good at appearing calm when my heart is pounding). Clearly, the baboons also knew me as an individual.[6] This knowledge was lasting, as I learned when I paid an unexpected visit to one of my study troops seven years after last being with them. They had been unstudied during the previous five years, so the adults had no recent experience with people coming close to them, and the youngsters had no such experience at all. I was traveling with a fellow scientist whom the baboons had never met, and, as we approached on foot from a distance, I anticipated considerable wariness toward both of us. When we got to within about one hundred yards, all of the youngsters fled, but the adults merely glanced at us and continued foraging. I asked my companion to remain where he was, and slowly I moved closer, expecting the remaining baboons to move away at any moment. To my utter

---

[6] I tested this once by dressing up a woman friend of similar appearance, height, and build in my field clothes. Carrying my distinctive hat, sunglasses, binoculars, and notebook, she emerged from my jeep and approached the baboons. They almost immediately took off, looking back nervously, even though she was still several hundred meters away. On another occasion, I returned after a few days' absence, with most of my long hair cut off. The baboons closest to me began to run away, but then they stopped, turned around, and peered at me intently. I could see the light of recognition dawn as, one by one, they relaxed and resumed their normal activities.

amazement, they ignored me, except for an occasional glance, until I found myself walking among them exactly as I had done many years before. To make sure they were comfortable with me, as opposed to white people in general,[7] I asked my friend to come closer. Immediately, the baboons moved away. It was I they recognized, and after a seven-year interval they clearly trusted me as much as they had on the day I left.

Trust, while an important component of friendship, does not, in and of itself, define it. Friendship requires some degree of mutuality, some give-and-take. Because it was important, scientifically, for me to minimize my interactions with the baboons, I had few opportunities to explore the possibilities of such give-and-take with them. But occasional events hinted that such relations might be possible, were I encountering them first and foremost as fellow social beings, rather than as subjects of scientific inquiry. For example, one day, as I rested my hand on a large rock, I suddenly felt the gentlest of touches on my fingertips. Turning around slowly, I came face-to-face with one of my favorite juveniles, a slight fellow named Damien. He looked intently into my eyes, as if to make sure that I was not disturbed by his touch, and then he proceeded to use his index finger to examine, in great detail, each one of my fingernails in turn. This exploration was made especially poignant by the fact that Damien was examining my fingers with one that looked very much the same, except that his was smaller and black. After touching each nail, and without removing his finger, Damien glanced up at me for a few seconds. Each time our gaze met, I wondered if he, like I, was contemplating the implications of the realization that our fingers and fingernails were so alike.

I experienced an even greater sense of intimacy when, in 1978, I had the exceptional privilege of spending a week with Dian Fossey and the mountain gorillas she had been studying for many

---

[7] The baboons were far more comfortable, in general, with white people than with Africans, simply because most of the whites they had known were nonthreatening researchers, while most of the Africans they'd encountered were local people who sometimes chased them.

years. One day, I was out with one of her groups, along with a male colleague unfamiliar to the gorillas and a young male researcher whom they knew well. Digit, one of the young adult males, was strutting about and beating his chest in an early challenge to the leading silverback male. My two male companions were fascinated by this tension, but after a while I had had enough of the macho energy, and I wandered off. About thirty meters away, I came upon a "nursery" group of mothers and infants who had perhaps moved off for the same reasons I had. I sat near them and watched the mothers eating and the babies playing for timeless, peaceful moments. Then my eyes met the warm gaze of an adolescent female, Pandora. I continued to look at her, silently sending friendliness her way. Unexpectedly, she stood and moved closer. Stopping right in front of me, with her face at eye level, she leaned forward and pushed her large, flat, wrinkled nose against mine. I know that she was right up against me, because I distinctly remember how her warm, sweet breath fogged up my glasses, blinding me. I felt no fear and continued to focus on the enormous affection and respect I felt for her. Perhaps she sensed my attitude, because in the next moment I felt her impossibly long ape arms wrap around me, and for precious seconds, she held me in her embrace. Then she released me, gazed once more into my eyes, and returned to munching on leaves. If you find this account hard to believe, watch Dian Fossey's National Geographic special on the mountain gorillas and look for the scene in which she comes face-to-face with the young male Digit (the same one whose macho display drove me away).

After returning from Africa, I was very lonely for nonhuman company. This yearning was greatly eased by my dog Safi, who, like the baboons, has given me the opportunity to experience a joyful intersubjectivity that transcends species boundaries. I turn now to this relationship, because, while few of us can travel to Africa to live with wild baboons, most of us have the chance to develop a bond with a member of another intelligent, social species, be it a dog, a cat, or some other kind of animal.

Before I went to Africa, I had lived with dogs, but not until my baboon experience did I begin to question the rather limited framework within which I, and other members of my culture, relate to our "pets." The very word "pet" connotes a lesser being than the wild counterpart, a being who is neotenous, domesticated, dependent. Even the most avid pet-lovers generally operate within a narrow set of assumptions about what their animals are capable of, and what sort of relationship it is possible to have with them. This was true of me before the baboons, despite my long experience with pets and abundant knowledge of animal behavior.

I rescued Safi, aged eight months, from an animal shelter where she had been brought as a stray, collarless, without history. She hovered on the border between childhood and adulthood, mature enough to focus her attention intelligently, but still extremely puppylike in demeanor and playfulness. From the instant of our first meeting, I experienced her as a wild animal[8] possessed by an instinctual wisdom akin to that of my baboons. Because I had so much respect for her intelligence, I did not consider it necessary to "train" her. Instead, I discuss all important matters with her, in English, repeating phrases and sentences over and over in particular circumstances to facilitate her ability to learn my language. She understands (in the sense of responding appropriately) to many English phrases, and she, in turn, has patiently taught me to understand her language of gestures and postures (she rarely uses vocal communication). Some dogs bark when they want to go out, but Safi instead gazes at the door, even if she's standing far away, and then looks at me (it took me a while to catch on). If we're out walking, and I become too absorbed in my own thoughts or in talking with other people, she regains my attention by gently touching her nose to the back of my leg in that sensitive spot behind the knee. As I write this paragraph, she

[8] This perception was no doubt facilitated by the fact that she closely resembles a jet-black timber wolf, her dogness given away only by the abnormally large size of her upright ears.

leaves the spot where she's been resting for the last hour and gently prods my elbow with her nose, signaling a desire to connect. When I approach her with a similar desire, she's nearly always willing to pause in her activities to attend to me, and I do the same for her. I stop typing, meet her gaze, say her name, and brush the top of her head with my lips. Apparently fulfilled by this brief contact, she leaves me uninterrupted for another hour or two, a restraint specific to those times when I am writing.

Through encounters like these, I have developed a deep appreciation for the subtlety and gentleness of her communication, and I have tried to respond in kind, by keeping my voice low and my touch soft, even in situations of great emotional intensity, for her or me or both. These situations are bound to arise when dogs live in a human-dominated world that carries dangers they may not understand (such as cars) and prohibitions that defy their instincts (such as not eating squirrels or chasing deer). For example, early in our relationship, we came upon several deer about a hundred yards away grazing in an open field. They were barely moving, but Safi had clearly caught their scent. One doe lifted her head and turned toward us. In response to this movement, Safi leapt forward (she was not on a leash). I said, without raising my voice, "No, Safi, don't chase." To my amazement, she stopped in her tracks. Thus I learned that I could communicate prohibitions without yelling or punishing her. I learned later that with Safi, rules do not have to be absolute. Under some circumstances, it's OK for her to approach a cat (for instance, one who is an expert on dogs), and more often, it's not. If I notice a cat nearby, before I open the door to let Safi out of the car (or disengage her leash), I say either, "No cats" or "It's OK to greet the cat." If I say the former, she turns her head away from the cat and walks with a bit of a slink in the other direction (as if avoiding temptation), but if I say, "It's OK," she'll check to make sure I mean it, and if I repeat myself, she'll approach the cat.

The most remarkable example of Safi's willingness to respond to my preferences concerning her relations with other animals involved a very tame, very fat (and very stupid?) fox squirrel who approached us, sat a couple of feet away, went up on his haunches, and chattered at her. I asked Safi to stay put. Her body trembled all over but she held her ground. The squirrel did too. I asked Safi again to stay put, and then I told her over and over how much I appreciated her self-control. The squirrel remained. Finally, I turned away and said to Safi, "Please come with me." She did.

These examples might be taken to indicate that I make and enforce the rules in our relationship, but this view is inaccurate, for two reasons. First, Safi has trained me in at least as many prohibitions based on her needs. For example, she has taught me that I must not clean the mud off her delicate tummy area with anything but the softest cloth and the tenderest touch. She has made it clear that stepping over her while she is asleep makes her extremely uncomfortable, and so I never do it. Second, Safi knows that absolute prohibitions are rare. More often, we find ourselves in situations in which I have one preference and she has another. Unless her safety or someone else's is at stake, we negotiate. For example, we have come to an agreement about the much-hated bath. I bring her into the bathroom and suggest that she climb into the tub. Usually, with great reluctance, she does so. But sometimes she chooses not to, in which case she voluntarily travels to the kitchen where she remains until the mud has dried enough for me to brush it off. Similarly, when playing fetch with a toy, Safi drops it when I ask her to only about half the time. If she refuses to drop it, it means either that she's inviting a game of keep-away, or that she wants to rest with her toy for a while before chasing it some more. Since the toys belong to her, and since she never substitutes objects like my new shoes, it seems fair that she decides when to keep the toy and when to share it with me.

I could sum up our relationship by saying that Safi and I are equals. This does not mean that I think we are the same; we are, in fact, very different, she with the blood of wolves in her veins, me with the blood of apes. What it does mean is that I regard her[9] as a "person," albeit of another species—a possibility first made

[9] And, equally important, she behaves as if she regards me as a person in the same sense of the word.

real to me during my life with the baboons. In the language I am developing here, relating to other beings as persons has nothing to do with whether or not we attribute human characteristics to them. It has to do, instead, with recognizing that they are social subjects,[10] like us, whose idiosyncratic, subjective experience of us plays the same role in their relations with us that our subjective experience of them plays in our relations with them. If they relate to us as individuals, and we relate to them as individuals, it is possible for us to have a *personal* relationship. If either party fails to take into account the other's social subjectivity, such a relationship is precluded. Thus while we normally think of personhood as an essential quality that we can "discover" or "fail to find" in another, in the view espoused here personhood connotes a way of being *in relation to others*, and thus no one other than the subject can give it or take it away. In other words, when a human being relates to an individual nonhuman being as an anonymous object, rather than as a being with its own subjectivity, it is the human, and not the other animal, who relinquishes personhood.

The possibility of voluntary, mutual surrender to the dictates of intersubjectivity constitutes the common ground that Aquinas and O'Hearne ignore when they claim that animals and humans cannot be friends. I use the word "surrender" intentionally, for relating to others (human or nonhuman) in this way requires giving up control over them and how they relate to us. We fear such loss of control, but the gifts we receive in turn make it a small price to pay.

Thus because I regard Safi as a person, and she regards me as one, we can be friends. As in any genuine human-to-human friendship, our relationship is predicated on mutual respect and reciprocity. Although she depends on me to provide certain necessities, like food and water, this dependence is contingent, not inherent; if I lived in the world of wild dogs, I would depend on her for food and protection and much more. She is not my child; she is not my servant. She is not even my companion, in the sense

[10] Cf. Elizabeth Costello on viewing animals as subjects rather than objects.

of existing to keep me company. I wish for her what I wish for all of my friends: maximum freedom of expression, maximum well-being.

So that Safi and I can experience the full joys of canine-being and primate-being, we spend a lot of time outside, moving freely. Most of the dog-walkers I know automatically decide where to go, and the dog accommodates. But because I spent years following baboons around, I realized that nonhumans tend to have a superior grasp of wild places. It was natural to transfer this attribution to Safi, and I made sure that she understood the words "You decide where to go," as well as "Please bring us back to the car [or house or camp]." Thus much of the time we are outside together, Safi, not I, determines where we go. Putting Safi in charge turned out to be a very good idea, because she reliably discovers more interesting places to go than I ever would: the beaver dam hidden behind the boulders, the secret stream at the bottom of the valley, found just as we are yearning for a drink.

Because Safi has considerable autonomy, she freely chooses many aspects of how she will relate to me. As a result, she does things for me that I could never have imagined and certainly could never have "trained" her to do. For example, at some point Safi apparently decided that when we're alone in the wilderness, whenever I close my eyes or lie down, her job is to remain sitting or standing, monitoring all directions continually. I discovered, in fact, that she will refuse to lie down or close her eyes, no matter how tired she is, unless I adopt an alert posture and tell her, expressly, that it is OK for her to rest (one of the many sentences she understands). Had I "trained" her to play this role, I would have to rely on her continued "obedience" to rest assured that I was fully protected. But because Safi chose this role of her own accord, presumably out of a deep regard for my safety, I trust her absolutely to continue to watch over me.

In our early months together, Safi appeared to prefer perfunctory pats to wrestling or snuggling, and she still does not relish the kinds of extensive physical contact that most dogs crave from the people they love. This aversion to cuddling makes all the more precious her behavior when I am feeling very low. First she approaches, looks into my eyes, and presses her forehead against mine. Then, without fail, she lies down beside me, maximizing contact between her body and mine. At this point, if I'm not already lying down, I do so (Safi has taught me that). As soon as I am supine, she rests her chin on my chest, right on top of my heart, and locks her gaze with mine until my mood shifts. Perhaps, a skeptic might respond, she does this simply because she's learned, first, that you're more fun when you're not feeling sad, and, second, that she can cheer you up in this way. To this I would reply: if we had human companions who behaved in much the same way, for identical motives, would we doubt their sincerity, or consider ourselves very lucky indeed?

I do not claim that any dog will show such behaviors if treated as an equal. In fact, I believe that Safi is exceptional, that she was born, perhaps, with an unusually sensitive nature. However, I do firmly believe—and my experience with other animals supports this belief—that treating members of other species as persons, as beings with potential far beyond our normal expectations, will bring out the best in them, and that each animal's best includes unforeseeable gifts.

What would Elizabeth Costello say to all this? I suspect she would not be surprised by my experiences with baboons or my relationship with Safi. Indeed, they seem very much in keeping with her claim that "there is no limit to the extent to which we can think ourselves into the being of another." But I would phrase her point slightly differently, so that it has less to do with the poetic imagination and more to do with real-life encounters with other animals. My own life has convinced me that the limitations most of us encounter in our relations with other animals reflect not their shortcomings, as we so often assume, but our own narrow views about who they are and the kinds of relationships we can have with them. And so I conclude by urging anyone with an interest in animal rights to open your heart to the animals around you and find out for yourself what it's like to befriend a nonhuman person.

CONTRIBUTORS

J. M. COETZEE is the author of seven novels (most recently *The Master of Petersburg*, 1994) and three volumes of criticism, as well as of memoirs and translations. Among the prizes he has won for his fiction are the Booker Prize, the Prix Femina, and the Jerusalem Prize. He is Professor of General Literature at the University of Cape Town.

WENDY DONIGER is the Mircea Eliade Distinguished Service Professor of the History of Religions at the University of Chicago. Her most recent book is *The Implied Spider: Politics and Theology in Myth*; forthcoming is *Splitting the Difference: Gender and Myth in Ancient Greece and India*. She graduated from Radcliffe College and received a Ph.D. from Harvard University and a D.Phil. from Oxford.

MARJORIE GARBER is William R. Kenan, Jr., Professor of English at Harvard University, and Director of Harvard's Center for Literary and Cultural Studies. A Shakespearean and a cultural critic, she is the author of seven books, including, most recently, *Dog Love* and *Symptoms of Culture*.

AMY GUTMANN, Laurance S. Rockefeller University Professor at Princeton University, is founding director of the University Center for Human Values. Her books include *Democratic Education* (Princeton University Press), *Democracy and Disagreement*, with Dennis Thompson (Harvard University Press), and *Color Conscious*, with Anthony Appiah (Princeton).

PETER SINGER is a Professor in the Centre for Human Bioethics at Monash University. He is the author of several books, including *Animal Liberation*, *Practical Ethics*, *The Expanding Circle*, and *Rethinking Life and Death*. From July 1999, he will take up an appointment as DeCamp Professor of Bioethics in the University Center for Human Values at Princeton University.

BARBARA SMUTS is Professor of Psychology and Anthropology at the University of Michigan. She is the editor of *Primate Societies* and author of *Sex and Friendship in Baboons* as well as numerous scientific articles on social relationships in wild primates and dolphins. She received a B.A. in Anthropology from Harvard College and a Ph.D. in Neuro- and Bio-behavioral Sciences from Stanford University Medical School.

INDEX